I0549158

THORPE'S CANDLE
A Matt Skyler Adventure

Joe Moore

Books by Joe Moore

THORPE'S CANDLE

Also by Joe Moore writing with Lynn Sholes

THE DESTINY CODE
BRAIN TRUST
THE TOMB
THE SHIELD
THE BLADE
THOR BUNKER (A short story)
THE PHOENIX APOSTLES
THE GRAIL CONSPIRACY
THE LAST SECRET
THE HADES PROJECT
THE 731 LEGACY
THE COTTEN STONE OMNIBUS
BAM! JUST LKE THAT (A short story)

THORPE'S CANDLE

© 2017 by Joe Moore
All Rights Reserved. No part of this book may be
reproduced or transmitted in any form or by any means,
graphic, electronic, or mechanical, including photocopying,
recording, taping, or by any information storage or retrieval
system, without the written permission of the publisher.
Any unauthorized usage of the text without express written
permission of the publisher is a violation of the authors'
copyright and is illegal and punishable by law.
This is a work of fiction. Names, characters, places, and
incidents are either the product of the authors' imagination
or are used fictitiously, and any resemblance to actual
persons, living or dead, business establishments, events, or
locales is entirely coincidental.

Published by Stone Creek Books
Oakland Park, Florida
www.stonecreekbooks.com
Interior design by Joe Moore
Cover design by Joe Moore
Cover photo by Michael Francis
Cover image © 2017
ISBN-13: 978-0692904244
ISBN-10: 0692904247

JOE MOORE

ACKNOWLEDGMENTS

Special thanks to my friends

Ken McGorry
James Glass

DEEP FREEZE

The North Atlantic, 1961

"We got trouble."

The words jarred Henry Bristol from his sleep. He looked up at the weathered face of the pilot. "What?"

"I said we got trouble." Chewing on a cigar, the pilot leaned over the makeshift seat in the back of the cargo bay where Bristol sat. "See that engine out there?"

Bristol glared out the window of the old DC-4. A black patch of oil streaked across the wing like a bloody wound.

"Pressure's dropping like a brick and we got a blizzard down there. Got to turn around."

"No!" Bristol's eyes widened. He was suddenly wide awake. "I already paid you. You assured me this plane could make it with no problem. I can't go back! Don't you understand?" His voice rose in pitch almost to the point of cracking.

"I think you're the one that don't understand. We can't make it on three engines with a payload this heavy. Got to turn around and find a place to put her down for repairs. Our best bet's Godthab, Greenland. Get the oil leak fixed—day or two at the most."

As the pilot turned, Bristol stood and grabbed him by the shoulder. "No! You must keep going." He was almost a foot shorter than the burly pilot and immediately realized his bad judgment.

The pilot balled his fist in Bristol's face. "Don't force me to explain it again, little man. Remember, you're not even supposed to be on this plane. Now park it and shut up." He shoved Bristol back into the seat, turned, and made his way between the large wooden crates until he disappeared into the cockpit.

Bristol felt the plane bank. There was no going back. As far as the world he left behind was concerned, he was dead. Dead and buried. He had to convince the pilot to change his mind. Maybe he could appeal to the man's greed. His foot nudged the duffel bag under his seat—so full of cash he could almost smell it.

He stood and pulled his coat around him. There was hardly any heat—another thing that annoyed him. Jumpy by nature, he looked around his surroundings with darting eyes, magnified through the thick lenses of wire rimmed glasses. Determined, he maneuvered past the rows of crates until he stood at the cockpit door. How much should he offer? What did it matter? He had to do whatever it took. Opening the door, he stepped inside.

The only other person on board was the copilot, a skinny man with beady eyes and a scraggly beard. He busied himself at the controls as the pilot turned to Bristol. "I told you to stay put."

Bristol took a hesitant step forward. "I'll pay you twice what we agreed."

"We're losing a hundred feet per minute." The copilot's voice was anxious.

"How can that be?" The pilot scanned the array of instruments. "What the hell's going on?"

"It's number two." The copilot pointed to a set of dials.

"All right, triple the price."

"Shut up!" the pilot yelled.

Bristol started to make another offer but the words never came. The DC-4 vibrated violently followed by a loud bang and the shriek of ripping metal.

"Oxygen!" the pilot called out and grabbed his mask. He turned to Bristol and pointed to an extra mask hanging over the vacant navigator's position. "Put it on."

Bristol grabbed the oxygen mask and shoved it to his face. The plane's nose dropped, and he saw the churning expanse of storm clouds ahead. "What happened?" His voice was muffled behind the thick rubber.

"Propeller blade," the pilot shouted. "Ripped off number two. Must have torn through the fuselage. We've lost cabin pressure." He shut down number two engine then keyed his microphone. "Mayday! Mayday! Godthab tower, this is Arctic Air Cargo 101. We've lost cabin pressure and two engines. Request emergency instructions. Godthab tower, do you read?"

"Nothing but static!" the copilot said while he adjusted the knobs and dials of the radio transmitter. "We're not getting through."

"Keep giving out our position," the pilot ordered as the plane plummeted into the clouds.

Like bouncing off a wall the DC-4 bucked and pitched, sending Bristol to the floor. He hit his head and felt blood flow down his face.

The tremors worsened as the pilot struggled with the controls. "I can't turn her, rudder's frozen. Propeller must have severed the cables." He ripped his mask off when the altitude needle passed the ten-thousand-foot mark. The plane tossed and rocked as it continued its steady drop into the belly of the storm.

"Get back to your seat and strap in," the pilot shouted to Bristol.

He turned to start back when the plane shook again. This time, he thought it would rip apart. Thrown forward, he smashed into one of the large wooden crates that filled the cargo bay. His head and shoulder struck with a crack, burning pain shot through his arm. Blood flowed into his eyes. He heard the wind scream across the jagged slash in the fuselage. Groping his way to his seat he swiped the blood from his forehead on his sleeve and grabbed the duffel bag.

When the plane broke through the clouds, Bristol glared out the window and saw what he thought were lights of a small town passing underneath. As quickly as they appeared, they were gone, replaced by a dense shroud of swirling white.

The DC-4 leveled off as if it were about to land. The pilot must see a place to put the plane down, Bristol thought. A cautious feeling of relief swept over him. Had the pilot heard the offer of more money? No. Too much noise and confusion. Bristol looked out the window again. For a precious few seconds a break in the storm revealed what looked like a vast colorless ocean with row upon row of giant waves frozen in place, stretching off to the horizon. What kind of nightmarish scene was this? Were his eyes playing tricks? Had the bump on his head caused him to hallucinate?

There was a rumble—must be the landing gear dropping into place. They were going to land! Bristol pressed his cheek against the cold window trying to see what lay ahead. The strange landscape rushed by—the white ocean got closer. Once they landed, he figured they could wait for the storm to pass then make their way back to the town. He would find a place to stay while the plane was repaired. A few days at the most, the pilot had said. A small price to pay for committing the perfect crime and getting away with murder. A reassuring smile crossed Bristol's lips. Strapping himself in, he wrapped his arms around the duffel bag, holding his breath.

Like a specter appearing out of a nightmare, Arctic Air Cargo 101 swooped down and glided in across the top of the Greenland ice cap. The driving wind of the season's worst blizzard had built up huge banks of tightly packed snow and ice. The instant the plane's front gear bit into the white powder, the nose rammed into a snow bank and the impact crushed the cockpit killing the pilot and copilot. Bristol's seat ripped from the floor. Still strapped in, he flew forward and collided with one of the cargo crates.

The old DC-4 groaned and shrieked as the snow swallowed it, the sounds of its agony nearly smothered by the roar of the blizzard. When only the tip of the tail stuck above the snowfield, the ripping and tearing finally stopped.

Dizzy and numb, Henry Bristol opened his eyes. In the fading glow of the cargo bay lights, all was finally calm and quiet—the howling of the storm now distant and muffled. He told himself that it was only a matter of time before a search party would come. He had always been a patient man. This time would be no different. Steam drifted up from the wound on his head as he hugged the bag and waited.

SKYLER

San Jose del Cabo, Mexico. Present day

The majestic *West Wind* sat in the heat, its twenty-seven-thousand tons towered over the berth at the docks of the small resort town. With a flurry of last minute activity, the final passengers boarded and the gangways retracted. Soon it would continue on its cruise to the next port along the western coast of Mexico. The ship's twin Sulzer diesels sent a constant low rumble through the waters of the channel. Gulls dove through the sky above the ship's gleaming chrome and teak appointments.

A few hundred yards away on the opposite side of the channel, a small outboard bobbed in the light chop, its presence all but ignored in the heat of the early afternoon. A teenage boy pretended to fish while he kept a close eye on the cruise ship. Halfway between him and the *West Wind* was the *San Felipe*, a Mexican government archaeological dive boat anchored in the middle of the channel. The boy watched as two divers surfaced, boarded the *San Felipe* and prepared to move it to allow clearance for the cruise ship to depart.

Cruise ships were a mainstay to the popular resort destination, and their prop wash had stirred up the bottom helping to uncover long-buried items. For the last two weeks the government-sponsored project had uncovered bottles, pottery shards, 19th century machinery parts, and rock ballast from early galleons. Many items were the result of a mid-1800's hurricane that demolished the town along with numerous ships. The deadly storm had uprooted many coffins from a cemetery near the beach. Old newspaper accounts told of people seeing coffins floating out to sea.

The boy waited patiently for the *San Felipe* to raise anchor and move up the channel. Having watched the same routine with other ships for three days, he knew he would have about twenty minutes alone at the dive site to search for any salable artifacts before the ship departed and the archaeologists returned.

When the *San Felipe's* engines came to life and it started moving north, he put on his dive gear and slipped over the side into the warm, dark water. The heavy throb of the cruise ship seemed to come from every direction. He followed the sloping side of the channel down until it leveled off, forming a muddy gray plane littered with chunks of coral and limestone. Odd-shaped pieces of debris stuck up from the sediment like partially unearthed bones.

Finally, the dive site appeared. The boy saw the outline of a grid system made of wires stretching between an angle-iron frame. The grid covered approximately two thousand square feet and lay suspended a few feet above the bottom of the channel. Numbers and letters on plastic markers dotted the grid showing the location of interesting finds.

He moved across the top of the grid looking for any items he could take back and sell to the less-scrupulous souvenir shops in town. To his untrained eyes however, everything looked the same—strange-shaped objects covered with a layer of neutral-gray silt. Tied to the wires in five or six areas were a few small orange plastic ribbons. He searched these first.

The closest ribbon marked the upper half of a large blue glass jar filled with liquid. A second marked the tip of an enormous timber running at an angle down into the sand. He swam from ribbon to ribbon fanning the silt away to reveal other objects.

The boy glanced at his dive watch. The only thing that concerned him was the departure of the ship. Being caught in its prop wash could be deadly—clearance was tight even at high tide. Once the ship started to move, he knew he would only have a few moments to get to a safe distance.

The pitch of the ship's engines rose as he stopped at the next ribbon. Again he fanned the silt. This time he saw the worm-riddled top of what was left of a large wooden box. It materialized out of the muddy bottom having been preserved under the thick layer of mud and sand. Brushing his hand across it caused a glint of light to reflect off a piece of metal—a small plate about 100 millimeters square. Engraved on it was the image of a tree. As the current washed away the silt cloud, the image took shape—a full oak tree that spread its limbs from a thick mature trunk.

He continued to run his hand across the plate revealing more of the image. Maybe he'd found something important, he thought, something the divers had missed! Then the words *En Memoria O Recuerdo De*, "In Memory of" appeared, and he knew in an instant that he was looking at the top of what was once a coffin.

As his hand jerked back, a dark shadow eclipsed what little light there was and threw the dive site into gloom. Just as suddenly, a tremendous blast of water shoved him head over heels across the top of the grid. His regulator caught in the metal wires and the force of the water slammed him into the angle-iron frame. He cried out with wrenching pain. Then his head smashed into an outcrop of limestone and his face mask cracked.

The drone of the ship's engines grew to a deafening pitch. Dazed and frightened, he lay trapped on his back looking up at the shape moving overhead. He tried to swim but the latticework of the grid held his tank in its tangled grip. Panic took hold as he squirmed about becoming even more firmly entangled. The immense thrashing sound roared in his ears as the whirling screws of the ship came directly at him.

~ ~ ~

Matt Skyler yanked his dive mask off and tossed it into a yellow plastic milk crate. His stomach ached from hunger and he regretted skipping lunch. The excitement of the morning discoveries had pushed him back into the water just as soon as he'd come up for a fresh tank.

At six-three, Skyler had a dark tan, an Olympic swimmer's body that filled every square inch of his black one-piece and long caramel-colored hair that hung in ringlets down his brow. He moved with a confident stride across the deck of the *San Felipe* to the bridge. Just inside was an ice chest filled with cartons of orange juice and two six packs of Corona. He grabbed an orange juice, downing half of it in three pulls. Next, he found a box of soda crackers kept in the map cabinet. Taking a handful, Skyler ate as he watched Paco Cruz kneel and inspect a small mass of wet purple rock covered with what was once a graceful anemone. Now it resembled a formless glob of spinach.

Skyler walked over to stand beside his fellow diver. "What do you think?"

Cruz poked the rock with his diver's knife. Then he looked up smiling. "It's definitely the handle of a sword, Señor Skyler. Mid-seventeenth century, give or take a decade. I believe we have found the *San Paulo*."

Slightly shorter than Skyler, Cruz had dark bronze-colored skin and the strength of a bull. His long black hair hung down his back as he stood and slipped out of his wet suit. Cruz was the government archaeologist from the Department of Mexican Antiquities in charge of the search for the illusive *San Paulo*. It had been a galleon loaded with ivory and jade that had burned and sank in the bay over 300 years ago.

"I cannot thank you enough, Señor Skyler, for giving up part of your vacation to come to my aid. If it were not for you, I would still be looking in the wrong place."

"Dumb luck, believe me." Skyler shrugged and bit into his last cracker. "Just remember, Paco, the deal was for a case of *Sauza Tres Generaciones* if we find the *San Paulo*."

"And so it shall be, my friend. You will have your tequila."

"Why don't we run one more survey just to be sure?"

"A fine idea. As soon as the cruise ship leaves, I'll program another sub-bottom profile." Cruz picked up the relic and gently placed it into a tank of salt water.

Skyler scanned the sleek lines of the *West Wind* as it prepared to move away from its berth. He watched the swirling dark currents created by the side thrusters stirring up the channel. Then he saw a small powerboat anchored across the waterway tossing about with no one aboard. He moved back to the bridge and grabbed a pair of binoculars. Focusing on the middle of the channel, he saw what he feared—the telltale trail of bubbles moving across the channel

"Damn!" Skyler turned to the man inside the cabin. "Captain, shut her down." Then he rushed across the deck and grabbed a fresh tank out of the storage rack. "Crank up the scooter, Paco!"

"What is it?"

"Souvenir hunter."

"Sweet Jesus, where?" Cruz tried to see what Skyler was talking about.

"This side of that outboard." He pointed as he slipped on his tank and weight belt.

Cruz nodded then jumped off the stern to the lower platform and unhooked the AquaBike, a small battery-powered underwater scooter used for hauling objects up from the bottom. "You only have a twenty percent charge. It may not be enough to get you there."

"Not much choice." Skyler dropped down beside him. "If I don't get that jerk out of there, he'll be sliced to pieces."

"Should we call the harbor police?" Cruz pushed the scooter off the platform.

"No time." Skyler slipped into the water and gripped the throttle. With a spray of foam, he disappeared under the chop.

~ ~ ~

The boy knew he had only seconds to live. Oh God, help me, he prayed as the dark monster swept over him. Suddenly, out of the blackness came a flash—the edge of a large knife sliced through his tank harness setting him free. A powerful arm wrapped around him. Then a hard rubber mouthpiece was shoved in his face and he took a deep breath. He felt himself being pulled across the top of the grid faster than he had ever moved underwater.

Within seconds, the screws of the ship passed over the point where he had been trapped and the dive site became an enormous cloud of silt and mud. The light grew brighter as he and his rescuer approached the surface. A moment later, they broke into the blinding Mexican sun.

The boy stared at the wall of metal that made up the *West Wind*. Only a few moments before it had been a leviathan of deadly proportions. Now it moved with grace and beauty along the channel heading for the open ocean, its multi-colored pennants dancing in the tropical breeze.

The thin, high-pitched whine of the underwater scooter buzzed in his ears as the low rumble of the cruise ship faded. The man who saved his life kept a solid hold across his chest while he steered the scooter toward the runabout. Once they pulled alongside, he let go and cut the power to the scooter. Almost immediately, the *San Felipe* appeared and maneuvered to within a few meters of the smaller boat.

"Señor Skyler, are you okay?" someone called from the dive boat.

Flashing a thumbs-up, the man helped the boy grab hold of the side of the runabout. "You gonna make it, kid?" he asked after pushing his dive mask onto his forehead and removing his mouthpiece.

"I think so." The boy's voice was choked and raw. His head throbbed from the impact of the rock. "Stupid, I guess."

"Stupid doesn't even begin to cover it. Diving alone is stupid. Being run over by a ship is downright insane. You really want to die that bad?"

"Forgive me, Señor, and *gracias*." He coughed as he held on to the bobbing boat.

"Take care of yourself, kid." The man patted the boy's cheek then flipped the power switch and guided the scooter toward the stern of the government dive boat.

With his remaining strength, the boy pulled himself into the runabout and turned to watch his rescuer climb onto the rear platform of the *San Felipe*. For an instant, the man glanced back at him and smiled—a smile that warmed him more than the golden Mexican sun ever could.

~~~

Skyler turned to Cruz. "What's say we call it a day, amigo? I've had it."

"I agree." Cruz swabbed the sweat from his forehead then secured the AquaBike onto the stern platform. "Do you think the young one learned his lesson?"

"Who knows? Truth is, that's just the kind of stunt I would have pulled when I was his age." Skyler dried his face on a towel and went to the ice chest inside the dive boat's cabin. This time he grabbed a Corona.

DEEP SCAN

Washington, DC

"Do you have any idea what you're asking me to do?" As he spoke, the President turned his back on the three men and stared out the window of the Oval Office. Dressed casually in slacks and golf shirt, he brushed his hand over his silver hair and watched the parade of tourists beyond the fences.

Dr. John Dolen answered. "Yes, Mr. President, we definitely understand." Dolen leaned forward in his chair with a determined expression. The tall, lanky, fifty-year-old nuclear research scientist from the Princeton Plasma Physics Laboratory had a narrow, stern face sporting a peppered gray goatee, thick horn-rimmed glasses, and small, dark eyes. "We would never suggest anything like this if we didn't believe it to be a matter of gravest concern. We simply don't see any other course of action. As Professor Reynolds and I have explained, we have reason to believe someone gained access, copied, and then destroyed the original Project Candle Power files. If that proves true and this technology should fall into the wrong hands, the United States and the rest of the free world would be helpless to defend against it."

The President moved to the leather chair behind the Resolute desk, his face pale and drawn. Only six months into his term and he already felt the accelerated aging process that came with the job. "Frankly, if it weren't for your impeccable scientific credentials and the insistence of Colonel Argentine, I would assume you both were raving lunatics."

"That's understandable, sir," Reynolds said. Professor Carl Reynolds possessed doctorates in both biochemical engineering and quantum physics from MIT. Short and stocky, also in his mid-fifties, he had a shiny, balding head and a warm smile. His chubby fingers constantly pulled at the ends of his bushy mustache. "To understand our concern, you must realize the nature of our organization. Deep Scan is one of a handful of ultra-secret projects unknown even to the CIA and National Security Agency. Even your predecessor didn't know it existed."

The President raised an eyebrow. "If that's the case, how do you get funding?"

"Actually," Reynolds said, "Deep Scan is a modern offshoot of the old Strategic Defense Initiative. As I'm sure you recall, the original concept of SDI was to create a defensive shield against a surprise missile attack from the Soviet Union."

"Star Wars had many levels," Dolen said. "Most were Level One projects that involved the military and the Department of Defense. Then there were Level Two projects controlled directly by the NSA dealing with offensive weaponry. Finally, there were a couple of Level Three groups like Deep Scan—purely scientific in nature, answering only to the President. President Bush, forty-three, conceived the idea of Deep Scan. He authorized Colonel Argentine's predecessor to set up a network of obscure research grants and bogus government agencies. They were buried deep in Washington's bureaucratic maze in places like the Department of Agriculture and the National Parks Service. Congress appropriated funds earmarked for everything from biological and chemical research to improving crop yields, farming techniques and fertilizer compounds. The funds really went for futuristic research into developing new energy sources."

"But that doesn't answer the question—why keep it a secret from the former administration?" The President directed the comment at Colonel Michael Argentine.

A little over six feet tall and lean with a straight nose, dark hair, and hollow cheeks, Argentine was a cognitive psychologist specializing in training techniques. Officially, the forty-five-year-old career officer served as director of the Institute for Defensive Research at the Southern Command Headquarters, Miami. Unofficially, he was the military coordinator for Deep Scan.

The colonel cleared his throat. "Well, sir, once President Bush created Deep Scan, he made arrangements for it to go on even after he left office. One of the last things he did was to instruct that the current President be informed about the existence of Deep Scan only if it were successful in its mission."

"I'm still not clear on exactly what that mission was, gentlemen."

Dolen spoke up. "The original assignment of Deep Scan was to evaluate existing military technology and adapt it to our nation's dependency on foreign sources of oil."

"About a month ago," Argentine said, "during a routine electronic file search through the Department of Defense archives, we came across a reference to something called Project Candle Power. It was only a partial document and our guess was it might have been a file fragment. It contained just enough information to attract our attention. Are you familiar with the principle of fusion, Mr. President, particularly the theory of cold fusion?"

The President nodded. "There were a couple of scientists in Utah—"

"Pons and Fleischmann," Dolen said.

"Didn't they claim to achieve fusion at room temperature?" the President asked. "But I thought the scientific community regarded their work as fake. Just a chemical reaction, not nuclear."

"Until recently it was never duplicated in other labs," Argentine said. "Even when there was success, it was inconsistent. Palladium is just too unreliable. But what we're talking about came prior to the Pons and Fleischmann experiments. Apparently, a decade earlier, the government conducted secret tests to develop an alternative energy source based on cold fusion. The tests were much more successful than what came later with Pons and Fleischmann in Utah."

"Obviously, it wasn't much of a success or there'd be a noticeable lack of gas pumps today," the President said. "So what happened?"

Dolen answered. "What started out as an energy experiment turned into the development of a new type of weapon, a weapon of unthinkable power capable of mass destruction on a global scale. It's referred to in the document as a korium device and was code named Thorpe's Candle."

"Interesting name." The President made a note on his pad. "Do we know how it worked?"

Dolen went on, "Yes, sir. To create conventional nuclear fusion, you need to operate in temperatures way beyond what can be safely handled in the lab."

"Like what you would find at the core of the sun," Argentine said. "One hundred million degrees or more."

"That's what makes cold fusion so attractive," Dolen said. "Theoretically, we're talking about very manageable temperatures and conditions. The theory of cold fusion is amazingly simple—a rod of metal such as palladium is placed in heavy water. Heavy water contains the hydrogen isotope tritium that is also an essential component of nuclear fusion weapons such as the hydrogen bomb. The palladium is placed near a second metal electrode and an electric current is applied to both poles causing electrolysis—the splitting of water molecules. Atoms of deuterium, a heavy isotope of hydrogen, are forced into the palladium metal where the deuterium atoms fuse to form helium atoms."

"My eyes are glazing over," the President said. "Can you give it to me in plain English?"

"I'm sorry, sir," Dolen said, blushing. "When the people working on Project Candle Power substituted the palladium electrode with one made of a rare mineral called korium, all hell broke loose. They came close to cooking themselves and everything in sight. There was heat produced in a factor of a hundred thousand to one, neutrons and gamma rays along with massive quantities of helium and tritium. All the makings of a nuclear event."

"Korium?" the President said. "Never heard of it."

Dolen said, "Korium has existed only in small quantities. Somewhat similar to platinum or rhodium, it was used for a short time for plating tiny precision instruments. There have only been a few sources of korium, mostly in remote areas of the Arctic. In fact, only one commercial mine ever existed. It was located in Iceland and played out after only a few years. According to the Department of Mining and Exploration, none are known to exist today."

"All right," the President said, "you've convinced me this korium is rare."

"Much more than rare," Dolen continued. "Essentially non-existent. That's why we theorize they abandoned Project Candle Power because there was no korium to build the device. Using anything else yielded minimal or no results—not worth the investment. The scientists destroyed their one working model and put their research data under Alpha level protection."

"So if there's no more korium, why are you so concerned about someone stealing the design of the device?" the President asked.

Reynolds answered, "Technology has come a long way since the discovery of cold fusion using korium, sir. Utilizing virtual elements created with the VR molecule engine at Lawrence Livermore, we've already confirmed that the device is possible. We can show in theory that Project Candle Power works using computer generated element simulations. All we need is a sample of korium to build and test the real thing."

"So this brings us back to the original problem," the President said. "You tell me that you've actually located a new source of korium but it's on foreign soil. And you want me to approve a covert mission to go in and get enough for you to confirm your tests?"

"That's correct, sir," Argentine said.

"Well, the suspense is killing me, gentlemen. What country are we talking about?"

"Since we uncovered the existence of Project Candle Power," Dolen answered, "we've had the Department of Reconnaissance reconfigure their RAYKR satellite to perform a search for any trace of the mineral. Yesterday they scanned the Caribbean. Their data confirms small traces of korium at a remote mining site in the mountains of Eastern Cuba."

The room fell silent as the President leaned back in his chair and stared at the ceiling. "Couldn't be someplace easy, I guess."

"No, sir," Argentine replied. "Never seems to work out that way."

"You said you believe someone else is working on a korium device. Do you think it's the Cubans?"

"We have no idea, sir," Reynolds answered.

"Well, if they're going to the trouble of digging it out of the ground, they must be doing something with it. Are they plating tiny precision instruments or are they building some new kind of hydrogen bomb?"

"There's no market for the mineral as a plating agent anymore," Argentine said. "There are too many other cheap, synthetically produced alternatives. I doubt the Cubans have the technology to construct Thorpe's Candle. Although cold fusion is simple in theory, it would still take a great deal of skill to set up a lab and build the device. We think they're extracting it for someone else."

Dolen added, "We're convinced that someone removed the files on the original Project Candle Power. Last night, Professor Reynolds ran a latent image sector and cluster scan and found that about six months ago the files were copied and subsequently erased."

"And the data could not be recovered?" the President asked.

"No," Argentine said. "It was electronically shredded at the highest security level."

"Could it have been a routine data purge?"

"Mr. President, data with an Alpha level classification can't be purged without an executive order from you or the National Security Adviser."

"Then how could it have been erased?"

"We don't know," Dolen answered.

"So," the President said, "along with everything else you've told me, we can also assume that someone has the ability to access the highest levels of secured files at the Department of Defense and do whatever they want to them?"

"It appears that way, yes," Colonel Argentine said.

The President shook his head and made a note on his pad to have the FBI start a full-scale investigation into who stole the file. Then he said, "Gentlemen, I've got a nationwide rail strike set to start at midnight, forest fires all over Southern California, and a budget crisis on Capitol Hill that's come close to fist fights on the Senate floor. I've got to tell you, this is not a good time to ask me to invade Cuba."

"Not an invasion, sir," Argentine said, "just a recon mission. A couple of Army Rangers and an Army Corps of Engineers mining expert."

"Are you absolutely certain that you can reconstruct this korium device?" The President's voice was stern.

"As certain as we can be, sir," Dolen said. "Based on our computer simulations, that is. What makes Thorpe's Candle so deadly is that its destructive power equals or dwarfs anything we currently have in our arsenal. Combine that with the fact that once you get around the technology, it's inexpensive to build. What was conceived as a cheap, renewable source of energy turned out to be a new way to produce widespread death and destruction."

There was a long pause before the President finally said, "If you had a supply of the ore, how long until you can deliver a working model?"

Argentine said, "It's hard to say at this point with so little data remaining from Project Candle Power. The important thing is to get our hands on a sample and start the real tests as soon as possible. In addition, it's imperative that we find and secure whatever sources of the ore exist in the world. We know someone has stolen the information. The possibility of this technology falling into the wrong hands is, well, too frightening to ignore."

The President stared at Argentine for a few seconds, then looked down at his notes. "Out of curiosity, why was it called Thorpe's Candle?"

"Apparently," Dolen said, "it was named after one of the original members of Project Candle Power, a brilliant young scientist by the name of Dr. William Thorpe."

"And where is this Dr. Thorpe now?"

Argentine answered, "He was a member of the chemistry department at the University of North Carolina for almost fifteen years. Then three years ago, his wife had a terrible bout with cancer. When she died, he became despondent and developed a heavy drinking problem. He went into debt, lost everything, and screwed up his career. The university finally let him go. The last anyone heard, he was somewhere in Mexico doing research for a pharmaceutical company."

The President thought for a moment then said, "How do you plan on getting your team into Cuba?"

"Navy sub," Argentine said. "We'll drop them off the southern coast of the island at night."

"Colonel, I'm authorizing you to use whatever resources you need to locate Dr. Thorpe. Get him on an Air Force jet back to your Deep Scan headquarters as soon as possible. No sense in re-inventing the wheel. I want him involved in the reconstruction of the korium device. In the meantime, proceed with your mission to Cuba. I'll expect a progress report every twelve hours. Understood?"

"Yes, sir."

The President stood. "For everyone's sake, gentlemen, I hope you're all dead wrong and this proves to be nothing but a waste of time." Without another word, he walked out of the Oval Office.

~~~

Dolen turned his silver Lexus out of the White House gates and onto Pennsylvania Avenue. "That was quite a gamble, Michael," he said.

"Maybe not," Colonel Argentine said. "More like a calculated risk." He watched the visitors ambling along the sidewalks admiring the splendor of the most powerful government in the world.

"Still," Reynolds added from the back seat, "it could have blown up in our faces. He could have rejected the whole thing and tossed us out on our impeccable behinds."

"I don't think so," Argentine said. "Here's his chance to go down in history as the man who saved the world from the most destructive force imaginable. How could he turn down a shot like that?"

"Let's hope you're right," Dolen said. He steered the Lexus toward Arlington, away from the crowds and monuments. "I don't want to be around when he finds out you sent your recon team into Cuba two days ago."

THE AZTEC PRINCESS

Off the West Coast of Mexico

C andice Stevens lay on the cool sheets, her mind drifting at the edge of sleep. She could feel the warmth of Matt Skyler beside her. From his breathing, she knew he was awake, probably staring at the dark ceiling of the stateroom. The scent of their lovemaking still lingered in the air. She felt a tingle of arousal as she considered turning over and making love again. How many times that night had she moaned with pleasure when he slid inside her and they moved as one in the darkness. She could not get enough of him. But he had so much on his mind. Candice smiled, knowing there would be many other nights.

That evening, she and Skyler had boarded the *Aztec Princess* for the last leg of their vacation. After he spent two days helping Paco Cruz find the *San Paulo*, she couldn't wait to get him back in her arms. At dinner, they had had one of their many discussions on why neither was ready to make a long-term commitment to their relationship.

They had met in Egypt three years ago. Candice had just finished photographing the layout for the *Sports Illustrated* swimsuit issue. She was invited to a lavish reception in honor of the President of Egypt at the Hotel Luxor near the banks of the Nile. As she stood talking to a group of international magazine editors, her gaze was drawn to a man standing alone in the middle of the crowd. He was tall and almost handsome—he would later describe himself as having a lot of rough edges. His skin was the color of someone who spent a great deal of time outdoors, and he needed a shave. Despite it being a semi-formal affair, he dressed in a suede sports jacket, jeans, boat shoes, no socks, and an open-collared, checkered shirt. She felt an instant attraction as she observed him. While the conversation rambled on with her friends, she watched him watching everyone else. His eyes moved from person to person with what appeared to be a sincere interest in each. When he noticed her stare, he returned it with a smile that made her feel she had known him forever.

"Who's the fashion statement?" she asked her friends.

"Matt Skyler, Director of OceanQuest," said the *National Geographic* science editor. "That's the guy that raised the Soviet sub off Bermuda. Helped to close a chapter from the last days of the Cold War. Received an accommodation from the Presidents of the United States and Russia. Among other things, he's one of the world's leading authorities on undersea military salvage. Been an adviser to *National Geographic* for years."

"What's he doing here?" Candice asked.

"I understand OceanQuest located an ancient Roman warship on the bottom of the Nile a few miles from here," the science editor said. "Skyler supervised the operation."

Candice excused herself and wandered over to stand in front of Skyler. "How's the treasure hunting business?"

"There's still a few to find." He smiled down at the petite photographer and offered his hand. "One in particular I'm anxious to explore. Matt Skyler, Ms. Stevens." They shook hands.

"I'm flattered that you know me, Mr. Skyler." She blushed not wanting to let go. "And what treasure might that be?"

"You of course. And call me Sky. All my fashion photographer friends do."

An hour later, they stood on the deck of the OceanQuest research vessel *Phoenix* anchored in the middle of the Nile. As a full moon lit the ancient river, their passionate on-again off-again relationship had begun.

~ ~ ~

Tonight's discussion with Candice on the cruise ship had ended the same way all the others had over the last three years, Skyler thought. No resolution but a great deal of sex.

Now wide-awake, he slipped out of bed.

"Everything okay?" Candice asked.

"Go back to sleep, sweetheart. Just going for some fresh air."

He found his khaki shorts and black Polo shirt where Candice tossed them after she undressed him. Stepping into a pair of boat shoes, he ran his fingers through his thick curly hair. A moment later, he stood in the corridor outside their stateroom.

At four in the morning the ship was unusually quiet. Matt Skyler strolled along the passageways with no particular destination in mind. An elevator came into view as he rounded a corner. At the other end of the hall, Skyler saw a steward in a white jacket moving a vacuum cleaner slowly over the red and gold carpet. Skyler entered the elevator and pushed the button marked Promenade Deck.

As the elevator ascended, he felt a throb in his head—a bothersome reminder of their relentless search around San Jose del Cabo for the perfect margarita. He hoped the night air would definitely do him good.

He stepped onto the windswept deck and he filled his lungs with fresh ocean air. Alone, he stared out at a moonless night. The stars washed across the heavens and glistened off the water. He thought of Candice and his unquenchable hunger for her. Yet he could never bring himself to ask her to give up her successful career. And at the same time, he just wasn't ready to settle down, start a family, stay in one place. Soon, their vacation would end and they would be off to different parts of the globe. When would he see her again? A week? A month? He missed her already.

A flash of light caught his attention. At first he wasn't sure it was there at all. He leaned forward and strained to see. A large object moved on a parallel course with the ship—it blocked out the reflected starlight. Skyler made out faint white lines of foam curling along its edge. His eyes adjusted and his pulse quickened. It was something he'd seen before on another night, another ocean. The low round profile with its slight humped back, the tall stark tower topped with antennas, and the tail fin that cut through the water like a shark's. There was no mistaking the distinctive profile of the Yankee-class Soviet nuclear submarine. It bore no markings, only a single black flag flying from the tower. Its insignia—a white skull and crossbones.

Skyler heard the clank of metal. He leaned over the rail and stared down the side of the *Aztec Princess*. A cargo door opened directly below him. Over the sound of the wind, he heard the buzz of an outboard motor. From the direction of the submarine, a small boat raced across the water. It maneuvered alongside the cruise ship and Skyler saw that it held two men. One kept the little boat steady while the other caught a half-dozen pieces of luggage flung from the cargo opening. One of the men yelled something that was lost to Skyler on the wind, and pointed at him. A man appeared in the cargo opening below and looked up. He waved the boat off then slammed the steel door shut.

What the hell was going on? Skyler thought. He rushed back to the elevator, but before he reached for the button, the doors opened. The steward he'd seen earlier stood inside, a club in one hand and a walkie-talkie in the other.

"We're going to collide with a submarine!" Skyler said and started to take a step forward. He had captained his boxing team at the Naval Academy and always felt he was ready for any punch. He never saw this one coming. The first blow slammed into his stomach. He doubled over, dropping to his knees. The second came down on the back of his head.

~~~

"Mr. Skyler?" It was a woman's voice. "Mr. Skyler, can you hear me?" It came from far away. He tried to move, to sit up. The back of his skull throbbed.

"Just relax," she said.

He opened his eyes. Everything hurt. "What happened?"

"You had a bad fall and hit your head. You may be dizzy for a while."

The room was white like the woman's clothes.

Then his memory started to return. "How long have I been out?"

"A few hours. Now I told you, relax."

"I need to speak to someone in charge." He tried to get up but the pain and dizziness stopped him.

The door to the small infirmary opened and a man dressed in a uniform entered. "How is your patient, Nurse Gomez?"

"He would be much better, Captain, if he listened to me and didn't try to move around."

"Captain?" Skyler said.

"Captain Santos, at your service."

"Are you aware that this ship came within a hundred meters of a submarine last night?"

"A submarine?" Santos chuckled, turning to Nurse Gomez. "Your patient has quite a sense of humor."

"I don't see anything funny in what I just said." Skyler held his head. "It would have taken only a tiny course change to have a major collision, Captain. You know the rules of distance between commercial vessels. Endangering your passengers is a serious matter."

"Mr. Skyler, you've had an accident. We're going to make every effort to treat your injury."

"Perhaps Mexican Customs authorities would be interested in knowing what your crewmen were off-loading to that submarine?"

"I have no idea what you are talking about, Mr. Skyler."

"So you're not aware that this morning, a submarine ran a parallel course with this ship and came within a hundred meters of your port side? A clear violation of international commercial steerage regulations?"

Santos gave Skyler a blank stare.

"I suppose you have no knowledge of the six pieces of luggage that were off-loaded to a small boat that pulled alongside? Check with your first officer, Captain. There's no way he could have missed it."

"You seem to know a great deal about ships, Mr. Skyler. Those are serious accusations. Let me try and get you some answers." He reached for a phone on the wall. "This is Santos. I want a report of any vessels that have come within fifty miles of this ship. Yes, midnight until seven this morning. I'm in the clinic." He hung up, turning back to Skyler. "I'm sure you believe what you're telling me, Mr. Skyler, but considering we found you unconscious, I must weigh the possibility that you were delirious. Perhaps you had a little too much to drink last night, passed out on the deck and hit your head?"

"Delirious? I know exactly what I saw. And when I went to report it, one of your crew attacked me. Then I woke up here."

"I can't imagine why any of my crew would attack you, sir."

The door opened.

"Matt, what happened?" Candice rushed to his side. She wore a purple jogging outfit. A sweatband held her dark brown hair in place.

"I'm Captain Santos," he said and stepped forward.

"Candice Stevens." She gave him a concerned look. Then she turned back to Skyler. "Are you all right?"

"I've been better."

"Your friend fell and injured his head," Nurse Gomez said.

"He's still a little confused," Santos added. "We recommend that he have x-rays as soon as we arrive in San Carlos Bay."

"Of course," Candice said.

"Nurse Gomez will be glad to give you the name of a clinic on shore if you like." The phone rang and Santos answered. He listened for a moment then hung up. "I think I can put your mind to rest, Mr. Skyler. Since midnight, we have come in contact with five vessels. The Puerto Vallarta to San Lucas ferry, another cruise ship, an oil tanker, what appeared to be a private ocean-going yacht, and a freighter who identified itself as Iberian registry. Of the five, the tanker was the closest—six-point-two kilometers."

"That's it?" Skyler sat up and swung his legs over the side of the examination table.

"Yes." Santos smiled broadly. "Now, I'm sure that answers all your questions. Please let Nurse Gomez know if there is anything else we can do for you."

Skyler started to say something but thought better of it.

Candice took his arm and they walked out of the infirmary. "What was that all about?"

"Something strange is going on, Candy." Still a little woozy, he leaned on her for support.

"They said you slipped and fell."

"I didn't slip. I saw something I shouldn't have and somebody knocked me out. Captain Santos knows what's going on. He's covering up the whole event. Besides, you can't miss a full-blown nuclear missile submarine."

"Missile submarine? What in the world are you talking about?"

"Not here." His words brought stares from a group heading to morning brunch. Back in their stateroom, he sat on the bed, rubbing his head. "It just doesn't make any sense."

"You've got to admit, Matt, a submarine is a little hard to believe."

"I know a Yankee-class when I see one."

"Then we have to report it."

"I did. You heard what the captain said."

"What if he's right?"

"Candy!"

"Okay, okay. It's just that you did hit your head."

"No, somebody hit my head."

"Calm down, honey, I believe you. But there is a chance that—"

"That I imagined it all? I didn't imagine anything and I didn't have too much to drink."

"How about all the margaritas?"

"I wasn't drunk. Either Santos is blind or he knows everything I've said is true. There's tons of electronic gear on this ship. No way could they miss that sub. What I need is some proof."

"Matt, relax. This is our vacation. You've told them everything. When we go ashore at the next port, you can make a full report to the authorities if you want. Until then, can't you just let it go?"

"I can't relax, I can't let it go. I've got to find out what was in those suitcases."

PEGASUS

The Caribbean, South of Cuba

"Where are you hiding, Mr. Bormann?" Mickey Gates asked himself as he propped his feet up on the edge of the video control console. He leaned back and rubbed his tired eyes—the stiffness in his neck didn't go away when he tilted his head from side to side. He glanced over his shoulder. Through the porthole he saw the moon rising above the slate-flat ocean.

Taking a sip of Red Stripe, Gates turned back to the high-definition video monitor. Like a doctor examining an x-ray, he scrutinized the wireframe, 3D-image profile of the ocean bottom. Somewhere down there was U-396. It had caught fire and sank on its way to South America in May 1945. Newly uncovered Allied documents contained evidence that Martin Bormann, private secretary and chief adviser to Adolf Hitler, had been on board fleeing Germany with a fortune in Nazi gold. After weeks of scanning hundreds of square miles of ocean bottom, the computer had yet to make a match to the U-boat's distinctive profile.

Enough for one night, Gates thought. He pressed stop on the digital video recorder. With beer in hand, he left the *Pegasus'* Video Analysis Center and stepped out onto the deck. The converted Coast Guard cutter lay at anchor on a calm ocean 70 kilometers off the east coast of the Yucatan Peninsula. Crammed with electronic gear, it was owned by OceanQuest, the undersea exploration company specializing in military salvage.

Gates strolled along the deck watching a school of kings break the surface thirty yards away. He was slightly less than six feet and solid as a load of concrete, his muscles fought to escape his pullover and shorts. He had a crop of dark shaggy hair, a chiseled square jaw, and moved with the confidence of a man who once competed on the U.S. Olympic wrestling team. His diving credits ranged from the gold-bearing rivers of the western United States to expeditions under both polar ice sheets. Reaching the door to the bridge, he stuck his head in and spotted Peter Jorg, the tall blond captain of the *Pegasus*. Jorg leaned over a table as he studied charts and entered coordinates into a computer. In his early thirties, Jorg had joined the OceanQuest team after finishing five years as an officer in the Swedish Navy. He wore a T-shirt that said, "OceanQuest divers do it deeper", a pair of denim cut-offs, and some well-worn boat shoes. "Mick," he said. "Burning the midnight oil?"

"Just going through the videos one more time." Gates walked over and looked at the computer screen. "Anything promising for tomorrow?"

"I wish I could say yes, but we've covered the same area so many times, I'm on a first name basis with most of the fish."

Gates glanced up at the white board. The last known location of U-396—20 degrees north, 87 degrees west—was written in large red letters. The Allies decoded the final flash message from the German High Command but it was buried in the mountain of post war documents for over fifty years. After the collapse of the Soviet Union, old KGB files were released and the last know position of U-396 along with its infamous passenger was discovered.

"Not that it'll probably matter," Gates said, "but just for grins, let's reverse the search pattern. Who knows, the scanning program might like looking at things from the opposite angle for a change."

"You're the boss." Jorg continued entering data. The phone on the bridge instrument panel chirped. Jorg walked over and answered. He looked up, smiled at Gates and held out the receiver. "It's Skyler."

Gates took it. "Sky, how's the margaritas?"

"They're fine, but nothing else is."

Gates heard the edginess on his best friend's voice. He knew Matt Skyler better than anyone. Outwardly, the former U.S. Navy Commander was adventurous and easygoing, somewhat conservative and unassuming. But Gates also knew the inner Skyler. If someone was unlucky enough to confront this part of him, they usually came up short. Cool and meticulous, Skyler rarely miscalculated when he set his mind to a task. He could also be moody and sometimes would withdraw to a place where even Gates could not reach him.

The two met in high school while racing dune buggies across the Arizona desert. Later, they both attended the University of Southern California and vowed one day to be in business together. OceanQuest was the result—two state-of-the-art research and exploration vessels funded by government contracts and in constant use around the world.

"You guys okay?" Gates asked.

"Yeah. Listen, Mick. I need you to check on a few things for me. Got a pencil and pad?"

Gates grabbed what he needed. "Shoot."

"Get into the COMNET database and see what you can find out about Aztec Cruise Lines. I want a full background check—who owns it, financial status, and complete history of the company."

"Got it. What else?"

"Call Dick Miller at the Pentagon. Remind him he owes me for saving his ass from being thrown in jail after that New Year's party in Washington. Then tell him I need to know the status of all Yankee-class boomers."

"I haven't seen one of those old tubs in quite a while."

"Me neither, until last night."

"It's late in Washington. Miller's probably gone home."

"Look up his private number in my database. Tell him it's important."

"Where are you staying?"

"Club Med, Sonora Bay. It's about twenty miles south of San Carlos. I'm flying back to Key West tomorrow. Candice is heading to New York. When I get home, I'll check in at the office first then have one of the guys fly me down in the seaplane. Save everything until I get there."

"You got it."

"How are things going on your end?" Skyler asked.

"Nothing yet. If we stay here much longer, we're gonna have to start paying Cuban property taxes."

"Well, don't give up, my friend. U-396's down there somewhere. She just knows how to hide better than most."

"So what's this Yankee-class stuff about anyway? Those buckets should all be scrap metal by now."

"I thought so, too, Mick."

"Anything to worry about?"

"Not sure yet, but once we hear from Dick Miller, we may all have a great deal to worry about."

~~~

"Now can we relax and have some fun?" Candice asked. The fashion photographer wrapped her arms around Skyler's waist and kissed his neck. "You've talked to Mickey Gates. He's hot on the case. You've reported everything to the police. They said they'd investigate. So there's nothing left to do but pamper and please me."

They stood in the small garden of their cabana and stared up at the moon rising over the distant mountains. Skyler could feel the heat from the desert that stretched beyond the protected, palm-laden oasis of Club Med.

"I'm sorry, Candy. I guess I have been ignoring you. Spending the afternoon at the police station was certainly a total waste of time. How about dinner by candlelight, champagne and a scrumptious dessert." He ran his fingers through her hair and brought her mouth to his. Her body pushed against him and caused an instant reaction—his cutoffs grew tight. As they kissed, she slid her hand into the front of his shorts quickly finding what made him so uncomfortable. He sighed as she wrapped her fingers around him.

"I want my dessert now," she said, and gave him a push back into the room.

"And spoil your appetite?" His words came with a shortness of breath as he dropped onto the bed.

"I'll take my chances."

Skyler lay on his back, arms outstretched. He felt a surge of passion as she unzipped his shorts, pealed his clothes away, and worked her tongue and lips over him. The warmth of her mouth drove him crazy, his breaths

41

coming quicker. He closed his eyes and moaned as she took him in her mouth, knowing from experience just what pleased him.

Suddenly, Candice pulled away. Skyler opened his eyes and looked up. Two men stood at the foot of the bed. One had Candice by the hair yanking her head back. The other pointed an automatic pistol at Skyler, its barrel extended with a silencer.

"What the hell is this?" Skyler realized he was not only naked but also fully erect. He started to get up but the man aimed the gun at Skyler's groin.

"Don't try it or you've just had your last hard-on."

Skyler recognized him as the steward from the ship, the one that had knocked him out. "Take your hands off her." He leaned on his elbows, his erection fading fast.

Candice's eyes filled with fear as the other man pulled tighter on her hair. "You're in no position to give orders. Do what I say and your girlfriend might live long enough to give you another blow job."

As the gunman pointed the pistol, Skyler kicked straight up hitting the man's forearm. There was a muffled pop and a slug slammed into the wall over the bed spraying chunks of plaster. Skyler dove at the gunman. The second man pushed Candice aside and brought his gun down across the back of Skyler's neck knocking him to his knees.

"You're a slow learner," the gunman said, and tapped the back of Skyler's head with the silencer. "Now listen carefully." He squatted to look into Skyler's face. "You've stuck your nose where it don't belong. Be a real smart guy and forget everything. Don't bother going back to the police. If they ask you any more questions, you tell them you were drunk, fell and bumped your head." He looked over at Candice. "It would be a real shame if something happened to her. A real shame." He turned back to Skyler.

"Understood?" He pushed against Skyler's nose with the end of the barrel.

Skyler said nothing. The second man brought the back of his hand across Candice's face. She fell against the wall with a yelp of pain—a trickle of blood appeared at the corner of her mouth.

"Understood," Skyler said through clenched teeth. He wanted to teach these men a lesson but he would do nothing to risk his lover's safety.

The men walked over to the open patio doors. "Have a nice day," said the steward from the ship. Then they turned and were gone.

"What's going on, Matt?" Candice asked, sobbing. "Who were they?"

"One was the guy that slugged me last night." He helped her to the edge of the bed. "I don't know who they are but you can bet I'm going to find out. Let's have a look." He examined her lip. "There's a small cut on the inside of your mouth."

Skyler got a wet washcloth from the bathroom and wiped the blood away. Then he pulled on his pants and shoes. "Lock the doors behind me."

"Shouldn't we call security?"

"No, not yet."

"Where are you going?"

"They paid us a visit, now I'm going to return the favor."

"Are you crazy? They'll kill you."

"Candy, they can't afford to kill me. I filed a police report. If something happens to me, it would confirm my story and bring the police down on top of the cruise line. No, they just want to scare the stupid American tourist so I'll go home and forget everything." He dug into the bottom of his travel carryall and removed a 9mm Beretta.

"I thought you left that at home," she said as she looked in the mirror and examined her face for any signs of a bruise. "Matt, don't go crazy. Those men weren't joking around."

"Neither am I." He checked the fifteen-round clip and stuck the gun in the waistband at the small of his back letting his shirttail conceal it. "Just lock the doors and don't let anyone in." He gave her a kiss on the cheek and walked out into the hot desert night.

~~~

"There were two men," Skyler said, standing at the entrance to the main Club Med building. "One medium height with dark hair, the other short and heavy,"

"Si, Señor," the young valet said after he brought Skyler's Jeep around. "They left just a few moments ago and headed toward San Carlos."

"What kind of car?"

"A Ford, Señor, a blue Ford sedan."

"Gracias." Skyler shoved a hundred-peso bill into the boy's shirt pocket. He hopped into the Jeep and headed north on the highway to San Carlos. The two-lane road wound along the edge of the desert toward the coast. Traffic was light and it took only a few minutes for him to catch up to the blue Ford. He followed at a respectable distance along the winding desert road. They passed an old Spanish mission and entered the outskirts of the small seacoast village. Most of the stores and houses were dark, the town already asleep.

The Ford pulled into the dusty parking lot of a cantina called El Toro, one of the few along the highway that was still open. Skyler slowed and steered the Jeep to the edge of the road. He watched the two men get out and go in the bar. Then he parked on the other side of the lot and turned off the engine. After a few minutes he walked over to the

Ford and tried the door. It was unlocked and he reached in and pulled the hood release. Opening it, he felt around until he found the ignition wires. He gave them a yank and then let the hood drop down quietly. Then he walked back to the Jeep and waited.

~ ~ ~

An hour later, Skyler saw the two men come out of the cantina joking and laughing, their words slurred, probably from a great deal of beer and tequila. When the Ford didn't start, the man on the passenger's side got out and lifted the hood. He leaned over and checked the battery connections. Then his fingers touched the dangling ends of the spark plug wires. He started to say something to the driver when the hood slammed down on his head. The other man looked up into the barrel of the Beretta.

"Get out slowly," Skyler said.

With a stunned expression, the driver opened the door and stood with his hands in the air. "You're making the mistake of your life," he said in a menacing tone.

Skyler walked over and searched under the man's coat. He found a gun and wallet.

"You got a lot of balls," the driver said. "You're gonna regret this."

Skyler shoved the Beretta into the man's stomach hard. He doubled over and dropped to his knees. Then Skyler heard a moan and raised the hood. Groggy, the second man tried to stand but quickly fell in the dirt holding his head. Skyler searched and found his gun and wallet too, and then he switched on the headlights. Returning to the front of the car, he flipped through the wallets. Each contained Colombian driver's licenses and a small amount of cash. Both had Bogota business cards.

"Okay Señor Llanos of the Colombian Tourist Council, want to tell me what was in the suitcases being off-loaded to the submarine?"

Llanos looked up still holding his head. "Go to hell."

Skyler leaned over. "Yesterday you were a steward on a cruise ship and today you're a Colombian government official. Looks like you can't hold a job, pal. Now I asked you a question and I want an answer."

"You'll be sorry for this."

"I'm already sorry I ever laid eyes on you two."

"You're not going to kill us," the other man said, finally able to breathe again.

"You're right," Skyler said, looking at the second card, "Señor Mendoza. I'm not going to kill you tonight. But if anything ever happens to Candice Stevens, if you ever get within a mile of her again, I'll blow your fucking brains out. Any questions?"

"No," Llanos muttered.

"Now hook the spark plug wires back up and get the hell out of here."

"What about our wallets?" Llanos said.

"Go back and tell whoever sent you to buy you new ones."

Mendoza fumbled around until he had the wires going to the right connectors. Skyler stood back while they got into the blue Ford. Llanos gunned the engine spinning the tires and spraying dirt as the car shot out of the parking lot. Once their lights faded in the distance, Skyler tossed their guns in a trash container. Then he went to the Jeep and headed back to Club Med. The hot desert air blew through his hair as he tapped Llanos' business card on his chin.

THE MINE

Sierra Maestra Mountains, Eastern Cuba

"There's a clearing and a road down to the right," said Captain Harper. He focused the binoculars on the lush green valley below. "That must be it."

A thousand feet up the side of the mountain, Harper, a mineralogist from the Corp of Engineers along with two Army Rangers watched from a concealed ledge. "No dust kicked up by any trucks, no smoke from their generators. Strange kind for a mining operation."

"No noise either," Corporal Brooks added.

Harper turned to Lance Corporal Ferguson. "Check it again."

Ferguson pressed a button on the STAR-LYNX module—a black box about the size of an external hard drive. A small, inverted, silver umbrella-shaped antenna fifteen centimeters in diameter extended from the top. A few seconds later, a number flashed on the red LED. "Reconfirmed, sir. We should be within sight of the mine."

"Well, it just doesn't look right to me." Harper wiped the sweat from his forehead. "And it doesn't help much being in this bug-infested shit hole. This is not what I had in mind when I joined the Corps of Engineers." He didn't mention his orders to search for any reference to something called Project Candle Power, whatever that was. And searching for korium seemed a waste of time. He figured that on the face of the earth, there was probably only enough to fill the bed of his F150.

"What now, sir?" Ferguson asked.

"It'll be dark in a few hours. We'll check it out then."

"It's time to send a fix," Brooks said.

"Do it." Harper continued watching the valley below while the Ranger entered a series of numbers on the STAR-LYNX numeric keypad and pressed the send button.

A hundred meters away, a Cuban soldier lay concealed in the underbrush. He focused his field glasses on the spot where he had just seen movement and watched it intently. Then, when he was certain of what he saw, he keyed his radio and whispered, "The Americans are here."

~ ~ ~

Harper slipped on his night vision goggles. Instantly the black jungle transformed into a surreal world of shimmering emerald green. He could see the flash of moth wings, and the gentle brush of the breeze across the tops of leaves made his surroundings come alive with movement. The damp smell of decay reminded him of the plant nursery he worked at in high school. He hadn't liked the smell then and he didn't like it now.

The gradual slope grew easier as Harper and the two Rangers moved down into the valley. He heard the sound of a small stream from somewhere off to his left. Insects buzzed constantly. After ten minutes, the men came to a single lane dirt track that ran like a jagged wound through the jungle. Harper checked the direction finder in his goggles heads-up display and pointed to the right. Ferguson and Brooks acknowledged with a nod. Then Corporal Brooks took his assault rifle from his shoulder and cautiously moved along the road, his boots crunching on the gravel surface. Harper waited until the soldier was about thirty yards in front of him before he followed. Ferguson brought up the rear.

An opossum waddled across the road ahead. Brooks paused the group until the animal disappeared into the jungle. Moving on for another ten minutes they finally came to a large, circular clearing about a hundred meters across, carved out of the jungle at the base of the mountain. To the right was a house trailer that probably served as the mining company office while to the left sat a military dump truck. A wooden building stood nearby that may have served as equipment storage. Lumber, chemical drums, pieces of plastic sheets, paper, metal, and garbage littered the area as if the crew had left in a hurry. On the far side of the clearing a pile of rocks stretched forty meters up the side of the mountain.

"Looks like we're too late," Brooks said when the others joined him.

Harper picked up a candy bar wrapper lying in the dirt and brushed away some ants. "Not by much. This hasn't been here all that long." He gazed around the clearing before pointing to the pile of rocks. "The mine entrance must be over there. Let's have a look."

They walked across the clearing. If the entrance was beneath the mound, Harper thought, it would take some serious equipment to dig it out. They'd come a long way for nothing. "I'm going to look around and see if there are any other openings to the mine. You two check out the trailer and the shack."

The Rangers headed back toward the house trailer while Harper investigated the pile of rocks. Finding nothing, he moved to the other side. Still nothing. He glanced over his shoulder to see Brooks and Ferguson standing on each side of the door to the trailer. While Ferguson covered him, Brooks reached for the handle and pulled.

Through Harper's night vision goggles, the fireball from the explosion seemed to take on the intensity of a super nova. He screamed as he covered his eyes. The shock wave slammed him against the rocks rupturing both his eardrums. The ground shook and caved in. He dropped into blackness and hit the bottom hard. Rocks and debris poured off the side of the mountain and covered the opening. In an instant, Captain Harper disappeared.

~~~

Dust and smoke filled the air as a Jeep came up the road and ground to a halt. Flames from the trailer lit up the clearing. Part of the floor and a portion of one wall were all that remained. Burning debris lay scattered across the clearing and into the trees on the far side. Captain Juan Ramirez, Regional Chief of Cuban Army Intelligence, along with three other soldiers, got out. Ramirez walked around kicking chunks of charred wood and twisted metal, and then turned to the soldiers. "Find the bodies," he said. "Then we can close this matter forever."

THE SEARCH

Captain Harper tasted blood in his mouth as he struggled to open his eyes—the lids felt like lead weights. He saw nothing but blackness, and he moaned from the pain in his chest and limbs. Harper reached out and touched cold wet rock. He found that he had fallen into a small crevice partially filled with water. With shaking hands, he examined his chest and arms—he was soaking wet. How much from the water and how much from his own blood, he couldn't tell.

A wave of nausea swept over him and he threw up. The muscles in his chest and stomach spasmed, and the pain from his ribs made him pass out.

~~~

Harper awoke groggy and confused. He crawled out of the water to a gritty patch of flat rock, coughing from the choking dust. Wiping the dirt and sand from his eyes, he tried to make out what was around him. Then he remembered the small flashlight in the leg pocket of his fatigues. Retrieving it, he held his breath and flicked the switch. The faint light barely penetrated the darkness, offering little comfort. He was suddenly aware of the night vision goggles hanging around his neck. Harper put them on and blurred green shapes materialized around him. He realized the auto-masking function had closed the electronic aperture within microseconds of the blast, saving his eyes. Thank God, he wasn't blind, he thought.

He tried to remember what had happened. There was a massive explosion. Was it an accident? No, the trailer must have been booby-trapped. But why? Someone wanted to hide something bad enough to kill for it. Were the explosives meant for him and the Rangers or any hapless person that came wandering along?

As a new wave of pain swept over him, Harper closed his eyes, drifting in and out of consciousness. When he awoke, he had enough strength to sit up and look around. Dirt and debris cluttered the mineshaft. A wall of rock and rubble blocked the entrance. He got to his feet and took a hesitant step before dropping to his knees. Again, the pain made him cry out. He figured he had lost a lot of blood and was probably bleeding inside.

Harper shook his head. "I'm not going to die in this filthy place," he swore. There had to be a way out, but he couldn't move the tons of rock covering the entrance. With only one other choice, he struggled to his feet, turned and limped into the blackness of the mine shaft.

~ ~ ~

"We've only found two bodies, sir." The soldier stood stiffly in front of Captain Ramirez.

Overhead, the clatter of a helicopter echoed across the valley as his men searched the surrounding jungle.

"I find that hard to believe. There was a great deal of dynamite, but certainly not enough . . ." He rubbed his hand across his neatly cropped beard. "Keep looking."

Ramirez returned to the Jeep and watched the activity around him. What a strange series of events, he thought. First the Koreans less than a month ago, now the Americans. What was so special about this place? So much secrecy coming from the highest levels. Normally his job was an easy one—rounding up a few rafters headed to Florida. But suddenly the Koreans came and reopened the old mine. They worked day and night for weeks hauling away a lot of ore before sealing up the entrance. Then there was word that the Americans might come, too. His orders were to set a trap and make sure there were no survivors. Headquarters needed confirmation that the mission was a success, that all were dead. He must radio in a report soon. Ramirez drummed his fingers on the dashboard of the Jeep. The body would turn up, he thought. They always do.

~ ~ ~

Harper adjusted the night vision goggles to their highest sensitivity. With the aid of the flashlight, they produced faint, blurred images. He still had to feel his way along the mineshaft. And what a primitive operation it was, he thought. Mining technology like everything else in Cuba was decades behind the times.

The shaft split—the way to the right inclined slightly while the left passage sloped downward. Harper tossed a mental coin, entered the tunnel to the right and followed as it snaked its way for hundreds of meters through the rock. Finally, he grew tired and stopped. Battling fear and pain, he lay down, closed his eyes and slept.

~ ~ ~

He awoke stiff and weak but soon managed to get up and continue. After an hour of slow progress, he found the shaft had split again. This time the right tunnel narrowed while the left branch disappeared into darkness. He could see definite signs that the one on the right resulted from an explosion. Renewed strength flowed through his body when he realized someone had blasted their way *into* the shaft from another passage. He moved into the narrow opening on the right, confident now that there was another way out.

~~~

The sun dropped behind the mountains and casted long, dark shadows down through the valley. Captain Ramirez was tired and annoyed—there was no trace of the third body. The light faded and he was running out of time. He must report to headquarters soon. So he paced back and forth with an urgency he hoped was not missed by any of his men.

Ramirez heard an approaching vehicle and stopped to watch a small four-wheel-drive pickup approach and park beside his Jeep. A man got out—Ramirez recognized Manuel Perez, head of the provincial mining office.

"Greetings, Señor Perez," Ramirez said as the man approached. "It is kind of you to come out so far into the mountains."

"What is this all about, Captain?" Perez was a tall, dark-skinned man dressed in work clothes. He wore thick glasses perched on a hawk-like nose. His voice had a high-pitched nasal quality that irritated Ramirez.

"An accident. We are looking for a possible survivor, someone who might be badly hurt. I called you because I hoped you could help."

"I will do what I can, but you seem to have plenty of men already."

"I did not ask you here to help search. I simply need information and you know this region well."

"True. I managed this mine for many years until it was shut down," Perez said. "What happened here?"

"Unfortunately, that is classified." Ramirez spoke with authority. "But whatever you can tell me about your operation would be helpful. Are there any places in the area where an injured man might go and hide? And is this the only mine in the valley?"

"There is nothing here but jungle, Captain. And yes, this is the only mine." Perez nodded toward the rocks covering the entrance. "Who sealed it up?"

"I'm sorry, but that, too, is classified."

"Could I have a look?" Perez asked.

"Of course." Ramirez motioned and they walked across the clearing. He glanced at his watch. Time was running out.

Perez took a few minutes to examine the area around the pile of rocks. Finally he looked up. "There has been a recent cave-in here. It appears that a small landslide covered the opening to the cave-in. It is possible that your missing man might be buried right here beneath our feet."

Ramirez stood beside him. Now that the mining engineer pointed it out, he could see what had happened. He turned to Perez. "Perhaps the mystery is solved, my friend."

"So you think the body is buried below?"

"A very good chance." At least that was what Ramirez intended to put in his report.

"Do you want me to bring in some heavy equipment and dig it up? I will tell you though, it would take a few days to do so."

"No need. It is better that this man be left buried here in peace."

"But what if he survived and is still alive?"

"No one could have survived the accident that took place here." Ramirez turned and led the engineer back toward the truck.

"You are probably right, Captain," Perez said. "And if someone did survive and was trapped inside the mine, it would be a long walk out."

Captain Ramirez froze, glaring at the mining engineer. "You told me this is the only entrance to the mine."

"No, Captain, I said it was the only mine in the valley."

"Explain."

"This area has a history of mineral extraction dating back many years. This mine has been opened and closed at least three times. The first was to bring out a small deposit of copper. The second, in the sixties, was for nickel. And finally a year ago, we opened it to search for korium."

"So there are other entrances?" Ramirez asked.

"I know of at least two. The oldest is about a half-kilometer to the east. The second is on the other side of the mountain. But it is an old mine, Captain. There may be others as well."

Captain Ramirez ran to his Jeep, his hands shaking as he grabbed the microphone to his radio. He knew that if he allowed the American to escape, his military career would not only end in disgrace, but probably with a bullet from a firing squad.

~~~

Just when Harper felt he could not take another step, he saw a light ahead, and he struggled forward. Rounding a turn in the tunnel, the passage ended and daylight came through cracks between planks and vines covering an opening. He pushed on the wood. Even in his weakened state, it took little effort for the old boards to fall away. Slipping off his goggles, he groaned as he pulled himself through the opening.

Harper breathed in the fresh clean air. The area, heavily overgrown, showed little signs that it had once been a busy work site. He spotted the remains of a road and stumbled toward it. Nothing had passed this way for years, he realized.

The sun was low to his right and the road lay straight ahead. He knew that if it continued in this direction, it would eventually take him to the beach where he and the Rangers came ashore—their small raft lay hidden among the dunes. With his remaining strength, he started forward and prayed that luck was still with him.

~~~

"No one has been here," Perez said. He shined a searchlight at the opening in the side of the mountain. Jungle growth hid the boarded-up entrance to the mine.

"We have made a bad choice," Captain Ramirez said, "and lost considerable time as well." He walked back to his Jeep. As he looked up at the first stars of evening, he said, "Take me to the other entrance."

GARGOYLES

Washington, DC

"I have two pieces of bad news." White House Chief of Staff, Nathan Templeton whispered into the President's ear as they smiled at the crowd of churchgoers and reporters. They stood beside the Episcopal bishop on the steps of Washington's National Cathedral. Behind them, fearsome gargoyles and stately flying buttresses formed an imposing backdrop for the weekly Sunday morning photo opportunity.

"It's always a pleasure, Mr. President," the Bishop said as they shook hands. "Our prayers go with you."

"Thank you, Your Excellency. I need all I can get." The President made a practice of attending services at a different denomination each week. As he spoke, he felt Templeton's hand touch his arm.

Flanked by Secret Service agents, the President waved to the crowd and moved down the steps of the cathedral to the limousine and the line of black SUVs.

"What have you got, Nathan?" The President settled into the back seat.

"It's what I don't have, sir. Any contact with Harper and the Rangers since yesterday afternoon."

"What's your best guess?"

"Captured or dead, sir."

"This is exactly what I feared would happen."

"I know, sir. I'm sorry."

"What's the second item?"

"It's Dr. Thorpe. If you'll remember, we were told he was last known to be working for a Mexican pharmaceutical company. It turns out that a Colombian drug cartel owns the company—it's a front for the production of illegal drugs. Thorpe disappeared about six months ago and is believed to be somewhere in South America working for the cartel."

"About the time the Project Candle Power files were copied and erased?"

"Exactly."

"I need you to brief the National Security Adviser so we can consider our options."

"I understand, sir."

The President stared out the window of the heavily armored Cadillac known as 'The Beast'. Then he said, "Do you think all this is just coincidence?"

"No."

LAST WORDS

The Caribbean, South of Cuba

"Dick Miller told me you were as drunk as he was," Mickey Gates said. "He didn't understand why the cops were only hassling him and not you."

"And he's right." Skyler took a sip of coffee. "It's all in who you know, partner." He had flown to OceanQuest Headquarters in Key West, and from there taken a sea plane to meet up with Gates on the *Pegasus*.

"Anyway," Gates continued, "Dick said the only Yankee-class boomers still around are part of the former Black Sea Fleet. After the collapse of the USSR, the Republic of Ukraine hung on to some of the subs as a bargaining chip to stay on equal footing with Russia. They eventually ran out of money so they had sort of a military surplus sale and got rid of them. Some of their customers were South Africa, North Korea, India, and a few South American countries. The Ukrainians removed all the missiles, but even those can be bought on the black market and fitted with conventional warheads."

"How comforting," Skyler watched the relentless Caribbean sun reflect off the ocean. They were sheltered from the heat in the Video Analysis Center of the *Pegasus*. The report was thorough as Skyler knew it would be. Like brothers, his trust in Gates went deep. On more than one occasion, that mutual trust had saved their lives. He turned to face his friend. "Last time I checked, none of those countries were flying the Jolly Roger. So what did you find out about Aztec Cruise Lines?"

"On the surface, it's legitimate. They're owned by an investment consortium out of Orlando called TexSys Financial."

"Doesn't sound too sinister so far."

"Agreed. So I dug a little deeper. Guess who their *numero uno* stockholder is?"

"I give up,"

"Banco de National, Colombia's biggest lender."

"Pablo Escandoza?"

"The one and only. He's never made any attempt to hide the fact that he owns the largest bank in the country."

Skyler rubbed his chin in thought. "So what's the connection between Escandoza and the sub?"

"No idea. I've looked at everything backwards and forwards and it still doesn't add up."

Backwards and forwards, Skyler thought. He stared at the coordinates of the German U-boat on the white board in front of him. "Mick, get me the transcripts of the Allied documents on U-396."

"What's up?" Gates pulled a loose-leaf binder from a shelf over the computer desk.

"You've given me an idea." Skyler paged through the document until he found what he wanted. "Here it is. Parts of the coordinates are backwards. It's not 87 degrees west, it's 78 degrees west."

Gates was already bending over the map table. "Or about 20 miles west of Niquero, Cuba."

"An easy mistake. Someone reversed the numbers when they decoded the old file."

"Must be why you get the big bucks." He marked the spot on the map with a grease pencil. "I'll notify Peter and the crew. We can be there in 24 hours."

Skyler walked out of the cabin and stood on the deck. He squinted from the glare from a cloudless sky. He might have solved one mystery, but an even bigger one remained. What was the connection between a mysterious pirate missile submarine and the world's most notorious drug lord?

~~~

"Here she comes," Gates said.

"I see her." Skyler watched the wire frame 3D-image moving slowly across the video monitor. "This part always amazes me."

Like a phantom from the shadowy depths, the computer-enhanced outline of the submarine's conning tower rose up from the bottom of the ocean. It sat slightly tilted at a curious angle almost as if questioning the electronic intrusion into its secret hiding place.

Gates keyed a series of commands into the computer and the satellite positioning coordinates flashed on the screen. "Nailed it."

Skyler pushed the intercom button to the bridge. "Peter, drop a sub-sonic marker."

"Done," Peter Jorg replied.

The image on the monitor grew more exact as the data banks in the computer compared and matched the known details of U-396 with the object resting on the ocean floor.

"Looks like she's intact," Gates said. "No visible structural damage, no breaks in the skin."

"She's sitting in some sort of narrow trench." Skyler watched the V-shaped walls form around the submarine. "Must be why no one's spotted her before now."

"I wondered that myself," Gates said. "Depth's only 50 meters. I'll bet thousands of vessels have passed over her."

"Yeah, but sitting at the bottom of that trench, you'd have to come at just the right angle to see her. And that's if you were looking for her in the first place."

Gates stood and rubbed his hands together. "This calls for a celebration." He moved to a small refrigerator near the bottom of the equipment racks and took out two bottles of beer. Twisting off the tops, he handed one to Skyler.

"We'll dive at first light," Skyler said after taking a long drink.

Gates turned the bottle up and swallowed half its contents. Then he said, "You think there's really Nazi gold down there?"

"If there is, we'll have to fight the Cubans over salvage rights. Our German permits only cover international waters. It'd be worth it though to finally find out whatever happened to Martin Bormann."

"You know, Sky, we should be detectives instead of salvagers."

Skyler nodded. "I've always believed that we're frustrated detectives trying to solve a murder mystery. The victim is usually a Spanish galleon and the murder suspect a nameless hurricane. The scene of the crime is the wreck and the evidence is usually scattered across the ocean floor. And the trail is always cold. The mysteries we try to solve usually happened hundreds of years ago."

"Sky?" A voice came through the intercom.

"Yeah, Peter."

"Something interesting. You and Mick might want to come up to the bridge."

"Be right there."

The two walked along the deck enjoying the cool easterly breeze. The moon was high overhead and starlight reflected off the water. Skyler detected the faint odor of vegetation. The jungles of Cuba were less than 32 kilometers away. "What's up?" he asked as they entered the bridge.

"Take a look." Jorg pointed to the High Definition radar screen. The *Pegasus* was clearly visible in the center of the display. He set the range indicator to half a kilometer and a small dot appeared drifting toward them.

"Go to phased array and ten times enhancement," Skyler said.

Jorg pressed a series of buttons and the dot grew into the shape of a small oval.

"Try a hundred times," Gates suggested.

The circle filled the screen and they could see the image of a man lying in what appeared to be a small inflated raft.

"Could be a refugee?" Gates said.

"Maybe, but he's on the wrong side of the island." Skyler leaned into the screen. "No movement, might be injured or sleeping."

"There's only one way to find out." Jorg moved to the ship's main control panel. He pushed the throttles forward and the hum of the twin diesel engines rose in pitch. The former Coast Guard cutter swung to port and cut through the black water. Skyler and Gates stood over the radar screen watching as the distance narrowed between the *Pegasus* and the small oval.

When the two images were almost touching, Jorg slowed the ship until it drifted on the current. Then the three went out to join the other crewmen on deck. One of the men took control of a spotlight and swung its beam across the water. They spotted the raft floating twenty meters away. Skyler watched his men work with flawless precision as they dropped a rope ladder over the side of the ship and scrambling down. When the raft came close, they grabbed it with hooks, secured it and placed the limp body in a rescue basket stretcher. Within a few moments, it was up and over the ship's rail.

"He's in bad shape," Skyler said as he searched for any signs of life. "There's a pulse but it's weak."

"Looks like he's been through hell," Gates said. He searched the pockets of the man's camouflage outfit until he found an I.D. "Not quite your typical Cuban refugee either. If you can believe his this, his name is Harper and he's a captain in the U.S. Army Corps of Engineers."

"Let's get him to sickbay," Skyler said. The group carried the man into the infirmary.

The only medical person on the *Pegasus* was Tom Bech, a former Army medic who was an acoustics specialist on loan from NASA to do underwater long-range communications experiments.

"What the hell happened to him?" Bech said when they laid the unconscious man on the examination table.

"We figure he tried to outrun a cattle stampede and lost," Gates said.

The medic cut away the filthy bloodstained clothes. Flipping on the examination light, he went over the body carefully.

"What do you think, Tom?" Skyler asked after a few minutes.

"He's running a high fever for starters. Bunch of cracked ribs and a fracture or two. Maybe a concussion and internal injuries. No way for me to tell. Both eardrums are ruptured. Some second degree burns from a fire or explosion. Not much I can do but fill him full of antibiotics and painkillers. He needs intensive care quick. I don't think he's got much time left."

"Peter," Skyler said turning to Jorg. "Call Guantanamo Naval Base. Tell them we have an injured man who appears to be a U.S. Army officer and we're steaming to their location."

"Right away, Sky."

"Tom, do what you can for him. Guys, thanks for your help." As the men filed out, Skyler stayed for a moment. Bech unlocked the drug cabinet and removed a vial of morphine. While he searched for a syringe, Skyler stood over the man lying on the examination table. One more mystery in a day full of unanswered questions, he thought.

Suddenly the man's eyes opened. His hand reached out and grabbed Skyler's wrist pulling him to within inches of his face. Bech's back was turned and didn't see the quick, silent motion.

The man tried to speak. Skyler moved closer until his ear touched the man's lips. Then he heard the words *korium device*. He turned and looked into the man's eyes. "What is a korium device?" he whispered.

The man's face contorted as he squeezed Skyler's arm harder.

Bech looked around. "You say something, Sky?"

Skyler bent low and listened to what seemed hardly more than the sound of light breathing. Each word was weaker than the last, each breath full of pain. Then just as suddenly as the man had reached out to Skyler, he let go and closed his eyes.

"Tom, quick! We're losing him."

Bech immediately started CPR. Soon Skyler took over but it was obvious there would be no reviving the patient. A few minutes later and with no response, they stopped.

"What did he tell you?" Bech asked as he placed a sheet over the body.

Skyler didn't hear the question. All he could think about was Harper's last words still racing through his head. *Korium device and Project Candle Power.*

EL DORADO

Bogota, Colombia

The priest adjusted his vestments for the third time and rearranged the small bottles of anointing oils. The young couple and their infant were late, and the priest was too busy to be kept waiting. So who were these people anyway? Who has so much influence that he was ordered by his monsignor to conduct the ceremony after hours when the church was closed to the public? His patience wore thin.

The smoke from the candles hung thick in the cavernous interior of the Cathedral Primada. Beams from the setting sun shone through the stained glass like transparent heavenly pillars. The Colombian Ministry of Antiquities was renovating the four hundred and thirty-year-old building. Scaffolding reached high into the dark overhead recesses. Preservation of the historical landmark represented a small symbol of stability in a country ripped apart by internal strife, government corruption, and open warfare between the military and rivaling drug lords.

The priest glanced at his prayer book again to confirm he had the correct section, the one on Baptism. He looked at his watch. Twenty minutes late. He would give them another five, and then he would lock up and go home.

"Good evening, Father."

The voice startled the priest. He jumped and spun around. His mouth dropped open as he stared into a face the color of ash. Cold black eyes looked blankly at him. Pale blond hair resembling corn silk hung down to the stranger's shoulders. The man's thin lips barely moved when he spoke.

Dressed in a black suit and white shirt, he said, "My apologies if I surprised you. I hope our tardiness has not put you to any inconvenience." He extended his hand. "I am Colonel Felix Blackstone."

The priest hesitantly returned the gesture and found the bony hand to have the warmth of a headstone. "Well, it's all right I suppose." His voice was shaky. "How long have you been standing there?"

"Long enough." He gave what the priest thought was a smile. Then Blackstone turned and nodded. From a side door, three men appeared followed by a young couple. The girl held a newborn in her arms. They came forward and stood by the baptismal fount. The mother smiled broadly and made cooing sounds at the tiny child. The father had his arm around his wife's waist and helped support the infant. The three men, each holding an automatic machine pistol, stood back as their eyes searched the empty cathedral.

"Are we ready to begin then?" the priest said.

"Soon." Blackstone picked up the small bottles of holy water and anointing oil and casually examined them. The mother continued to play with the baby while the young father beamed with pride as he looked down on his handiwork.

Then a side door opened. The priest saw a man walking toward them. Standing 5' 10", barrel-chested, and slightly heavy-set, the stranger wore a gray silk suit and open collar shirt. Under a head of bushy brown hair was a youthful face. The priest guessed the man's age at mid-forties. He walked with a slight waddle and his smile revealed a solid but stained set of teeth. He repeatedly brushed his hair out of his eyes. The priest recognized him as the notorious drug lord, Pablo Escandoza.

"Forgive me, Padre," Escandoza said, "but I'm always running late these days." He shook the priest's hand. "I'm sure God will accept my grandson into his fold even if I am never on time." Then with a quick brush of his hair, he nodded to Blackstone.

"Now we can begin," the colonel said.

~~~

A light rain fell as the limousine pulled away from the curb and headed along Avenida Jimenez through the center of the city. Escandoza glanced over his shoulder to see his daughter, her family and bodyguards get into their limo and blend into the downtown traffic in the opposite direction. Colonel Blackstone sat in a backward-facing seat and stared into the rain patterns formed on the dark bulletproof glass. Sitting beside Blackstone, talking on a cell phone, was Teresa Castillo. Escandoza watched her, his eyes drifting from her dark hair that fell around her shoulders to the flawless skin of her arms and finally to her long, bare legs flowing out of a short skirt. He trusted her completely to run his personal and financial affairs. She was a brilliant corporate attorney who had worked for him for over five years. Sadly, he thought, no man including himself would ever have her—her lovers were all women just as beautiful as she.

As Teresa spoke in hushed tones, he glanced at Blackstone. Unlike Teresa, Escandoza trusted Blackstone for a totally different reason—he paid the former Soviet naval officer incredible amounts of money to do whatever was needed. Blackstone was a mercenary on a world class level. His fees rivaled the budgets of many third world countries but he always delivered whatever he was commissioned to do. Blackstone would be there as long as the money kept flowing into his Luxembourg accounts.

Teresa ended the call. "The rumors are spreading about the Korean freighter lost in the typhoon with the Cuban korium shipment. Everyone is demanding assurance that we have another source and can still deliver the final product."

"I don't blame them." Escandoza brushed the hair from his eyes. "With the amount of money at stake, I would be getting nervous, too."

"Also," Teresa added, "General Cho landed an hour ago. He's on his way to Lake Guatavita."

"Let's see how he justifies having the lab in North Korea without any korium," Escandoza said.

"How are the Americans reacting to losing their men?" Blackstone asked, keeping his eyes on the rain on the glass.

"According to my sources, they have not tied together the Cuban mine and the lost Korean freighter." Teresa directed her answer at Escandoza. She never bothered to hide her distaste for the Colonel. "But it is only a matter of time before they do. Their satellite surveillance will show the freighter leaving the port in Santiago de Cuba two weeks ago."

Escandoza said, "The Koreans can't reveal what was on that ship, and the Americans can't talk about it either or the press would start asking questions. Next thing you know, someone would find out about the existence of their Deep Scan and Project Candle Power. The can of worms, as they say, would be opened wide."

"And our operation?" she asked.

"A setback, admittedly. It is a shame the ship went down in a typhoon. Not much you can do about that. We'll just have to go to our alternate source, won't we, Felix?"

"I have already started assembling a recovery operation," Blackstone said.

"I hope we haven't bitten off more than we can chew," Teresa said. "We're sitting on a fortune in sales and no product to deliver."

"Don't be so pessimistic, my dear. Remember that our customers are standing in line to place an order. This is just a minor delay. They will be patient, I assure you. The rewards outweigh the delay a thousand fold. Once we recover the alternative source of the ore, we will take over production of the devices, something we should have done in the first place."

"And if the Koreans object to having the lab in Colombia?" she asked.

"They have no choice. Dr. Thorpe works for me, not them. The lab goes where I say he goes. They'll just have to trust us."

"The Communists don't think that way," Blackstone said. "They thrive on mistrust."

"Then so be it. The bottom line is, they no longer have a say so."

"But if they agree to let us complete the production here," Teresa said, "won't they insist on supervising the operation?"

"Perhaps, but they will be in my back yard operating under my rules."

"And if they try to double-cross us?" she asked.

Escandoza reached out and patted her tanned knee, his eyes sparkling. "Then we chop their little yellow slant-eyed heads off."

CHO

Lake Guatavita, Colombia

"You're looking well, my friend," Escandoza said as General Cho Dal-Yun entered his office. The North Korean was a small, dapper man in his mid-fifties with bush-cut hair. Dressed in civilian clothes, he smiled as they shook hands.

"You of course know my Financial Counsel, Teresa Castillo, and my Director of Special Operations, Colonel Felix Blackstone."

The general nodded to Teresa. He glanced at Blackstone who sat on a couch paging through a copy of *Guns and Ammo*. Motioning the officer to sit, Escandoza then settled into a high-back leather chair behind a mahogany desk. Simon Bolivar, the great liberator of Colombia, once used the piece of furniture. The office was inside Escandoza's headquarters, a fortified underground bunker he fondly called "The Keep" after his favorite horror movie. It was located north of Bogota in the Andes Mountains near Lake Guatavita. Legend had it that centuries ago, El Dorado, the mythical Amazon king, coated himself in gold dust, sailed out to the middle of the lake on a golden ceremonial barge and bathed in the cool mountain waters. When the DEA proclaimed Escandoza the most wanted man in the world, and Forbes Magazine declared him the richest, the press started referring to him as the new El Dorado. To celebrate his notoriety, he coated his nude body in cocaine, sailed onto Lake Guatavita in a boat laden with the white powder and swam in the waters of his ancestors.

Escandoza's office was decorated with colorful Indian art, an extensive collection of pre-Colombian pottery, and a mix of paintings by some of Colombia's best-known contemporary artists. "What progress has been made on locating and recovering the korium?" he asked once everyone was seated.

"Our freighter passed through the Panama Canal twelve days ago and headed west." Cho said. "It was caught in a typhoon mid-journey. The last communication stated that the vessel was floundering and the captain ordered the crew to abandon ship."

"What are you going to do to find it?" Teresa asked.

Cho gave her a quick glance. Escandoza knew the General was not used to having a woman address him with such casualness.

"The area where we think it went down would take weeks to search. We have neither the manpower nor the technology. We believe the ship and its cargo are lost."

"We don't have weeks. Our buyers grow impatient," Escandoza said. "They have already started calling. A few have asked for their deposits back."

"What do you intend to do?" Cho asked. His voice was not as assured as before.

"You are going to move your lab and technicians here to Lake Guatavita. I will take over its management and security. Nothing changes but the location of the lab. Your scientists will build the devices and I will handle sales and distribution."

"This is not negotiable." Teresa asked.

Escandoza enjoyed the obvious irritation shown by the General each time Teresa spoke.

"The korium is lost," Cho said. "First we must search for another source."

"Colonel Blackstone is doing just that." Escandoza motioned to the mercenary.

"Any progress?" Cho asked without turning around.

"My operatives have discovered an obscure source," Blackstone said. "I will know more in a day or two."

"Where is it and how soon can we get it?" This time Cho swung around to face the mercenary.

"It is located in a remote area near the Arctic Circle on the Greenland icecap."

Escandoza swept the hair from his eyes. "Retrieving it will present a considerable challenge, but one that the Colonel is more than capable of, isn't that so, Felix?"

Blackstone diverted his eyes from the pages of the magazine for only a second, then continued reading.

"You know I cannot approve this without the Chairman's permission." Cho almost rose from his chair.

"Then get it," Escandoza said harshly. "In the meantime, prepare to set up the new lab here. As I said, our customers are starting to doubt our ability to produce a product. We must do something to calm their nerves. I am going to have Colonel Blackstone arrange for a simple sales demonstration."

"How can you do that?" Cho asked. "The korium is at the bottom of the Pacific Ocean."

"We have the original sample taken from Cuba. It is enough to construct one Candle, maybe two. What I have in mind will convince our customers that our product is well worth waiting for."

"Do you think it wise?" Cho asked. "Why show our hand to our enemies before we are ready to deliver the merchandise?"

"Because, General, we have two newcomers to the party—a Neo-Nazi group from South Africa, and our old friends in Iran. But because of the freighter sinking, they are sitting on the fence, to borrow an American saying. If they place an order, that brings our total to ten billion dollars. As far as I'm concerned, it's worth the risk for an additional two billion."

"I must remind you that we are equal partners in this operation," Cho said. "Do nothing until I discuss it with the Chairman. I feel it is a risky move."

"Discuss it all you want. But for two billion dollars, I plan on a convincing demonstration and I don't intend to wait long."

"What will you do?" General Cho asked.

"Let's just say it will be like wishing on a star."

The room fell silent for a moment. Then General Cho said, "There is another matter."

"Which is?"

"Our agents have discovered that the individual who witnessed the drugs being off-loaded from the cruise ship happens to be the Director of OceanQuest. He carries a great deal of weight with the U.S. government and has already started stirring the pot about the existence of a functioning nuclear missile sub."

"His name?"

"Matt Skyler."

"Is he a threat?"

"Possibly. He has a reputation for solving problems."

"Colonel Blackstone," Escandoza said, brushing the hair from his eyes. "Are you familiar with this man?"

"No, but he will be easy enough to locate."

"Fine." Escandoza gave the mercenary a nod. "Then when the time is right, kill him."

KEY WEST

Skyler watched a great white egret in the courtyard below his office. The bird danced a series of strange gyrations in a frustrated attempt to attract a mate. Skyler felt frustration, too, but for a different reason—he had found scant information on the mineral korium, and nothing on a korium device. And he discovered very little new info to what Dick Miller at the Pentagon reported about the current status of Yankee-class nuclear subs. Massaging his neck, he sipped coffee while gazing at the ocean through breaks in the trees.

Skyler's office was near the corner of Emma and Geraldine streets in Key West. Often when tourists left the Mel Fisher Maritime Museum and headed to the Ernest Hemingway Home a few blocks away, they would stop to admire the stately colonial home. Beyond the stonewall surrounding the estate, they could hear the soft clicking of the sprinklers that nourished the lush, manicured lawn all year round. It's landscaping of yellow hibiscus, purple bougainvillea and royal palms made for a beautiful photo. Few noticed the array of communications antenna and satellite dishes mounted on the roof, hidden behind giant ficus trees. A wrought iron gate kept the public out and a bronze plaque was the only clue to what lay inside. It read: OceanQuest World Headquarters.

"Morning, Sky. Welcome back."

Skyler turned to face Amanda Byrne. "Hi, Mandy. You been keeping everyone in line while I was gone?"

"Doing my best." The twenty-year-old college intern majored in Marine Biology at Florida Atlantic University and had elected to earn extra credit by working at OceanQuest over her summer break. She wore a red pullover, cutoff jeans and tennis shoes. Her blond hair was tied in a ponytail and her sunglasses hung on a strap around her neck. She carried a clipboard under her arm. "Are you back for a while?"

"Hard to say. There are a lot of loose ends to tie up on this submarine incident."

"I'm sure sorry to hear about the assault and your injury on the cruise ship." By this time Amanda had maneuvered her way into Skyler's office.

"Thanks." He nodded with a half-hearted smile. "I heal fast."

"So where is your girlfriend these days?"

"Candice is doing a fashion shoot in Istanbul. She'll be back in a couple of weeks." He knew exactly where the conversation was going. Amanda had a crush on him since she came to OceanQuest.

"I was thinking," she said shyly. "Maybe we could stop for a beer or something after work sometime?"

"Great idea. Spread the word around the office and we'll get a whole group together."

"Right." She dropped her shoulders. "I'll mention it." Then she said, "What are you working on so early? Anything I can help you with?"

"Only if you're an expert on a mineral called korium."

"I vaguely remember the name from chemistry class, that's about all. What's so special about it?"

"I don't know, Mandy. But it's important enough to be the last words of a dying man. I've gone through the research records of every major university with no luck in finding a scientific or government user. Now I'm letting the database compile a list of possible commercial users, past or present."

Amanda looked at the computer terminal. "I think it's done."

"That was quick." Skyler stood beside her. As he read the screen, he felt Amanda move closer so their arms touched. The message read: Search Complete. Press Enter for results. A single name appeared: Niagara Technologies, Buffalo, NY.

"That's it?" she asked.

"I guess so." He scratched his two-day-old stubble. "Mandy, see if you can get the number for Niagara Technologies."

She pulled her cell phone from her back pocket and asked Siri for the number. A moment later, the automated iPhone assistant responded, "No Niagara Technologies listed in Buffalo, New York."

He scratched his beard again. "Ask for any listing under electroplating."

Mandy read the results. "Just one, a company called Iroquois Metals. I'll text the info to you."

Skyler looked at his watch—too early to call. "Mandy, what's say we go over to the Blue Heaven for breakfast. When we come back we'll see if anyone in Buffalo can tell us anything about korium."

She beamed as she trailed him out the door.

~~~

"Iroquois Metals. Thank you for holding."

"Hi, I'm Matt Skyler with OceanQuest in Key West, Florida. Could I speak to the owner?"

"One second please."

While he waited on hold, he listened to an instrumental version of "The Long and Winding Road".

"This is Jimmy Nighthawk."

"Yes, I was holding for the owner."

"You got him. What can I do for you?"

"I'm Matt Skyler Director of OceanQuest in Key West. We're a marine salvage company"

"I've heard of you, Mr. Skyler. Among other things, you raised that Soviet sub off Bermuda."

"It was a group effort."

"So what can I do for you?"

"I was wondering if I could ask you a few questions?"

"Shoot."

"What can you tell me about a rare mineral called korium. In compiling a list of commercial users, we found a company called Niagara Technologies in Buffalo. They don't seem to be around anymore. Have you heard of them? Anything you can tell me about Niagara Technologies would be most appreciated."

"Not much to tell, they're out of business."

"Oh, how long ago?"

"My father bought out the company back in the sixties."

"I see. Well, actually I was interested in the type of work they did. I understand using rare minerals was their specialty."

"True, and that's what got them into trouble. I hate to cut you off, Mr. Skyler, but I'm running late for a meeting. If you want, you can jot your questions down and email or text them to me."

"I've got a better idea. I'd like to come up and talk to you personally. How about if I drop by and we chat?"

"Suit yourself. It's a long way to come for nothing."

"Could we meet tomorrow? I promise I won't take much of your time."

"Like I said, suit yourself."

"Great. How about 10:00 a.m.?"

"That's fine."

"Thanks, see you then." He ended the call and turned to Amanda. "Looks like I'm going to New York."

NIGHTHAWK

Skyler arrived in Buffalo late that night and checked into the Airport Hilton. Next morning he rented a car and was at Iroquois Metals by nine fifty-five. After waiting in the reception area for a few minutes, he was shown into Nighthawk's office.

"I'm Jimmy Nighthawk."

"Matt Skyler." They shook hands. "Thanks for seeing me on such short notice."

"How about a cup of coffee?" Nighthawk motioned.

"Sounds good." Skyler pulled out a small note pad from his shirt pocket as he sat down.

Nighthawk buzzed his secretary and ordered two coffees. He was a rugged looking man in his fifties with a proud, square jaw, lean face, black hair, and a hard, athletic build. Dark, piercing eyes seemed to evaluate Skyler. Trophies of fish—trout, bass, pike—all fresh water, all big, covered the walls of his office.

"Quite a collection," Skyler said as he glanced around.

"My passion. I can't wait until my son takes over the business full time so I can get out of here and spend the rest of my days on the lake."

Skyler nodded.

Nighthawk cleared his throat. "I must say your call yesterday aroused my curiosity."

"Really? Why is that?"

The coffee came and Nighthawk waited until the girl left. "Well, it's been years since anyone talked about Niagara Technologies. Now all of a sudden, is seems like everybody wants to know what happened to them."

"I don't understand."

"You're the second inquiry in less than a month."

"That right? Mind me asking who the other was?"

"Two guys. Said they were from a South American Importing company."

"No kidding?" Skyler said. "You don't happen to remember their names would you?"

Nighthawk rummaged through his desk drawer. "Here is one of their business cards. They came in about a month ago. Llanos and Mendoza, Cartagena Import & Export." He passed the card to Skyler.

The goons in Mexico, Skyler thought. He handed the card back but jotted down a note to have Mickey Gates do a background check on Cartagena I&E. "So anyway, tell me about Niagara Technologies."

"Not much to tell. They did a lot of government contract work during the fifties mainly plating microscopic scientific instruments. They pioneered a new technique using the mineral you mentioned."

"Korium?"

"Yeah. They got a huge government contract and were bringing a shipment in by air cargo but the plane went down in a blizzard somewhere in the North Atlantic. It was never found, and since there was no other source of the stuff, eventually they went out of business. Couldn't fulfill the contracts."

"Where did it go down?"

"Greenland, I think." He went to a file cabinet. Sorting through it, he pulled out a folder and returned to his desk. "Yes, Greenland. A two-week search was conducted but no trace of the plane was ever found. The flight originated in London with a stop in Iceland to pick up the ore. Entire shipment was lost." He took out a cargo manifest and handed it to Skyler.

"How did you get this?"

"We kept all of Niagara's old records."

The yellowed paper had Arctic Air Cargo printed across the top. As Skyler read, the total weight notation caught his attention—five thousand pounds. "Could I get a photo copy of this?"

"Sure." Nighthawk buzzed his secretary and asked her to come in. She took the page and left.

"So Iroquois Metals bought Niagara?"

"Right. My dad was running Iroquois at the time and when Niagara folded, he decided to make them an offer for the property and machinery. All he really wanted was the land. He auctioned the hardware and tore down the buildings. Sold the property ten years later for a sizable profit. There's an outlet mall there now."

"Can you tell me anything more about the nature of the work Niagara was doing for the government?"

"Not really. Like I said, it was mostly scientific research stuff. The few people I knew that worked out there never talked about their jobs. But there is someone who can tell you all about it. Fellow by the name of Harry Penn. He was a government scientist who managed the place."

"Where can I find Mr. Penn?"

"He's retired now, owns a small hotel near the Falls. Penn and his wife run the place. It's called the Colonial Inn. You should drop by and talk to him."

"I'll be sure and do that." Skyler stood as the secretary came back and handed him the copy of the manifest. "Thanks again for your time, Mr. Nighthawk. If you're ever in Key West, give me a call and we'll go out on the flats hunting bonefish."

"Count on it," Nighthawk said, and they shook hands.

Once Skyler left, Nighthawk picked up the Niagara folder to return it to the cabinet. A small piece of paper fell out and he bent to pick it up.

A memo.

Like the manifest, it was yellowed and faded. He didn't recall seeing it before. He read it, returned to his desk, and read it again. Then he looked at his watch. Five hours difference, he thought. He hesitated, then picked up the phone and dialed. There was a slight hiss from the overseas connection. Three rings later a young female voice with a heavy British accent answered, "Gordan Insurance Company, London branch."

"Hello, I'm calling from New York. Do you possibly have a Mr. Walter Smyth there?"

"Oh, you mean Chief Inspector Smyth. One moment and I'll connect you."

There was silence and then a voice said, "Smyth, here."

"Ah, yes, Mr. Smyth, I'm sorry to bother you. My name's Jimmy Nighthawk and I own Iroquois Metals in Buffalo, New York. I'm not sure if this applies to you but I recently came across a document in our company archives. It's from a Walter Smyth dated April 6, 1971. It says that if anyone ever inquires about the lost Arctic Air Cargo flight, we should give Walter Smyth at Gordan Insurance a call.

Does any of that make sense to you? I mean, have I got the right Walter Smyth?"

There was a long pause and a heavy sigh. Then the voice said, "Yes, you've got the right man. I've waited a long time for this call, Mr. Nighthawk."

THE SERVANT

Communist Party Headquarters, Pyongyang, North Korea

The General Secretary gazed across the table in the private dining room at General Cho. They had finished their meal and were ready to discuss business. A servant had removed the dishes and offered both men green tea. He then stood by in case either man requested anything else.

"So they have found another source of the ore?"

"Escandoza says it looks promising, Beloved Leader." Cho had arrived from Bogota only a few hours before and came to report personally to the General Secretary of the People's Republic of North Korea.

The long hours of travel the last few days had taken their toll on Cho, the General Secretary thought. The old soldier looked tired. "So he wants us to send our scientists to Colombia to finish the project?"

"Correct. And as long as Dr. Thorpe is under his control, I see no other way to proceed."

The General Secretary brooded as he stared across the room at the post-war Korean tapestries. Having the lab within the borders of North Korea would have made the korium devices assembly go quick. Now he must turn over the operation to a bunch of pirates and drug smugglers while the West is breathing down his neck to renew weapons inspections. Fortunately, they have no idea what the whole story is. They suspect he is building a weapon but they don't realize to what ends he will go to use it. Still, the setback gnawed at his gut.

He was running out of time. Each day, the South relied less and less on the Americans for protection. And because of the new trade agreements, their economy grew ever stronger. South Korea was becoming just another arm of the West. And he knew there were many in his own government that would never allow him to develop the korium device. They were brainwashed by the moderates and their American friends. They called themselves Communists, but in reality they were soft and weak, corrupted by the West. Just like the Russians and the other former Eastern Bloc traitors. Just like the Vietnamese, now wallowing in a capitalistic quagmire, forgetting the lessons of the past.

He was not going to allow this to happen to his beloved Korea. He would seize the opportunity to place a firm grip on his leadership before his enemies could harm him. With the money he would raise from the sale of the korium devices, and the power he would wield from possessing the deadliest weapon ever made, his enemies would stand back and tremble. But he must be cautious, there were those who would want him dead or at the least, locked away. He must remain totally in charge, possessing a power that the entire world would respect and fear. The korium device would give him the power he needed to unite the two Koreas.

"My sources tell me that the individual who witnessed the offloading of drugs onto the submarine is probing into places he should not be digging."

"Escandoza has promised to eliminate the leader of OceanQuest. But precious time is slipping by while we wait for the drug dealer and that renegade colonel to find the second source of korium."

"There will be enough time, Comrade General. Be assured that when the Americans finally realize what we are doing, it will be too late. We and our comrades-in-arms around the world will have our new weapons placed in the heartlands of America and its allies. They will have no choice but to step aside and let us do whatever we desire." The General Secretary studied the tea leaves in the bottom of his cup. "The clock is ticking, Comrade General. The day is soon coming when there will be one Korea—a Korea united under a common flag, the flag of Communism. It will be a sweet victory indeed."

"And what of the Colombians?"

"They are simply pawns in our global game of chess. Essential, but a pawn just the same. Believe me, Comrade General, when the time comes, I will deal with them just as I have dealt with the rest of our enemies."

"And if Escandoza suspects betrayal?"

"There is a saying: To defeat your enemy, bring him gifts through his front door so he will not hear death slipping in the back."

~~~

After the General Secretary and General Cho left the dining room, the servant finished cleaning the table. He brought in a new arrangement of flowers and set the table for breakfast the following day.

His work shift had ended so he gathered his belongings and made his way through the quiet hallways lined with the General Secretary's favorite paintings and silk screens. He emerged into a courtyard on the south side of Communist Party Headquarters, nodded to the guard at the security gate, and stepped out onto the sidewalk. A few blocks away, he stood under a lamp and watched the city lights reflect off the Taedong River. He paid no attention to the clatter of traffic and the bells of passing bicycles. Soon he noticed a woman and a young girl approaching—the girl sang softly to a small doll she held.

When they were close, he turned and smiled at the little girl, and bowed to the mother. The servant asked to see the doll and the girl handed it to him. He commented on how beautiful it was as he bent to give the girl a kiss on the cheek. Handing the doll back to the child, he again bowed to the mother, wished them a good evening, and watched them walk away.

Then he took one last look down at the dark, slow moving river before heading to his apartment a few blocks away.

THE INN

Skyler mulled over the events of the past week in Mexico and off the coast of Cuba as he headed west on Saunders Settlement Road toward Niagara Falls. He wondered if he was getting closer to finding any answers at all.

Near the entrance to the Tuscarora Indian Reservation, he saw the sign—Colonial Inn, A Bed and Breakfast. Driving up the gravel entrance road lined with sycamores, Skyler parked his rental beside two other cars. Firs and willows surrounded the old mansion, and a wide landscaped lawn gently sloped down to a lake with a dock and boathouse.

He grabbed his bag from the back seat and walked up the steps and across the front porch. Freshly painted rocking chairs and porch swings waited for guests to sit and enjoy the warm, sunny afternoons.

The lobby had polished wooden floors and paneling— the room brimmed with an impressive collection of Victorian antiques. A number of pictures of the Inn hung on the wall. There was no one behind the front desk so

Skyler took a moment to admire the photos. Then he heard someone approaching.

"She was built in 1838."

He turned to see a tall woman in a bright summer dress and sandals walk across the lobby. She had long, curly white hair and hazel eyes that smiled. Her slender face was slightly tanned with a hint of freckles, and she moved with the grace of someone who might have been trained as a dancer. He guessed her age to be late fifties.

"The Inn has quite a history," he said.

"Yes, it does. It once served as an army headquarters. And Theodore Roosevelt was sworn in as the twenty-sixth President right over there in the library." She extended her hand. "I'm Lilly Penn, and you must be Matt Skyler."

"Hello, Lilly." They shook hands.

"How long will you be staying with us?"

"Just for tonight. I'm flying to London tomorrow."

"Well, we're happy to have you." She went behind the front desk. "Things are a little slow right now so it's nice to see a new face." She opened the registration book and handed him a pen. "Your room will be number ten, just up the stairs to the right."

"Thanks. I understand you and your husband run the place. I was wondering if he was around? I'd like to have a word with him."

"Of course. Did you see the boathouse when you drove up?"

"Yes."

"That's where you'll usually find Harry. He has a little shop down there, makes fishing flies. It's his hobby. He sells them in town at the bait and tackle shops."

"I've been known to do some fishing. Maybe I'll buy a few flies from him while I'm here."

"He'd be proud, I'm sure. Make yourself at home and go down to the boathouse whenever you feel like it."

"Thanks again, Lilly."

Skyler went up the stairs, found his room, and dropped his bag off. He then headed out the back of the Inn toward the dock. The gravel path wound through flowerbeds filled with daffodils, zinnias and tulips. Evergreens and a well-trimmed hedge outlined the flower gardens. A gentle breeze from the lake swayed the tulips.

He walked down along the dock and opened the door to the boathouse. Inside was a room filled with fishing gear—the walls were covered with rods, reels, nets, and dozens of pictures of proud fishermen holding up their catches. Beyond a screen door, Skyler could see an old Boston Whaler tied up. An elderly man sat in the back of the shop bent over a workbench. He had a full head of silver gray hair and wore a checkered shirt, brown pants and Timberline boots.

Without turning around, he said, "Come in, Mr. Skyler."

"Thanks, but how did you know my name?"

"Intercom." He tapped a plastic speaker box beside him. "My wife let me know you might be paying a visit." He laid his tools down and turned around. "Welcome to the Colonial Inn, I'm Harry Penn." They shook hands. "Understand you're a fishing enthusiast."

"Saltwater mostly. I'm from Key West. I own a company called OceanQuest. We specialize in military salvage and deep water research."

"Did some deep-sea fishing myself while I was down in the Tampa area. Caught a lot of snapper about twenty miles offshore—one of those charter drift boats."

"I assume you like freshwater?"

"That's right. Granted, the fish are smaller but they've got a fighting spirit you just don't find in ocean fish. Unless you go hunting for one of those big bill fish."

Skyler picked up a fly. "A bucktail. Beautiful workmanship. Real deer hair?"

"Absolutely."

"You must sell these as fast as you make them."

"I have a pretty loyal clientele." With a sweep of his hand he motioned to the pictures covering the wall. Then he pulled a red bandanna out of his hip pocket and blew his nose. "Damn allergies. So what did you want to talk about, Mr. Skyler? Directions to the best fishing holes in the area, maybe?"

"Actually, I was interested in a company you once worked for—Niagara Technologies. I understand you were the general manager. I'm trying to get some information on a mineral called korium and my research tells me Niagara Technologies was a principle user the early sixties."

"You're correct. Unfortunately there just wasn't that much of it to be had. Eventually we lost our government contracts because of its scarcity, and a lot of bad luck."

"You mean the cargo plane crash?"

"Yes. Everything was fine until that shipment of korium went down somewhere in the North Atlantic. Then things fell apart after that."

"You must have done some interesting work at Niagara."

"Oh, nothing all that exciting. Mostly electroplating."

"So when Niagara folded, you retired?"

"I wanted to, but Uncle Sam insisted on keeping me around. Moved out to Texas in the mid-seventies to do some research for the government."

"More electroplating?"

"Alternative energy experiments."

96

"I take it you weren't successful?"

"I'm afraid that's something I can't discuss."

"Are you saying it's still classified even after all these years?"

"Nobody's told me different."

Skyler paused for a moment. "Who's using korium today?"

"Nobody, Mr. Skyler. It's all gone. So no one could be using it, now could they?" Penn turned back to his workbench and started winding a new fly. His irritation was obvious.

Skyler moved around to the side of the bench so he could watch the old man's face. ""Have you ever heard of something called Project Candle Power?"

Penn's hands tensed. He wiped his forehead with the bandanna. "You know, Mr. Skyler, it's getting hotter every day. Summer's here for sure." He looked up. "What's this got to do with fishing?"

"Let's just say I'm fishing for information."

Penn gave out a nervous laugh. "At least you're honest. How long will you be staying with us?"

"Just for tonight."

"I've got to finish these bucktails and get them up to O'Grady's before noon. Maybe we'll chat after dinner."

"I'll look forward to it."

"Fine, then you won't mind excusing me so I can get my work done?"

"Not at all."

Skyler walked out of the boathouse following the path back to the Inn. He heard the constant droning of bees as they moved through the flowerbeds. Nothing like exposing a raw nerve, he thought.

~~~

Skyler spent time on the phone checking on the latest developments covering the events in Mexico, the mineral korium, the current whereabouts of Yankee-class subs and Cartagena I&E. He also spoke with Mickey Gates who was in route from the *Pegasus* to OceanQuest headquarters.

After talking with Gates, Skyler called Dick Miller at the Pentagon. Miller said he had never heard of anything called Project Candle Power, and korium was one of those "ium" words he'd managed to forget from high school science class. Finally, Skyler called a contact with Scotland Yard in London and found out where to start looking for records of the search and rescue attempt and last known transmissions of Arctic Air Cargo flight 101.

At dinner that evening, Skyler enjoyed a home cooked meal of baked pork chops, fried potatoes, candied carrots, and iced sun tea with a generous helping of cinnamon bread pudding and whipped cream for desert. There were only a handful of others in the dining room—an elderly couple who told their waitress they had spent their honeymoon at the falls fifty-two years ago, a middle-aged couple visiting from Canada, and a retired college professor touring historical landmarks in the region.

Skyler saw no sign of Lilly or Harry Penn during the meal. The waitress said it was unusual for them not to come down at dinnertime to chat with their guests. After dinner, he wandered through the lobby and out onto the front porch. Skyler chose a big wooden rocker and sat back watching the fireflies dance across the front lawn. The evening air was cool and dry, the stars just beginning to cover the sky. After a few minutes, someone approached. He turned to see Lilly Penn coming toward him. She stood by the railing, her back to him, arms crossed.

"Who are you?" she asked.

"I've told you who I am, Lilly. Is there a problem?"

"There certainly is." She turned to face him, her eyes burning with anger. "I don't know what you said to Harry but I haven't seen him this upset in ages."

"Upsetting him was not my intention. I simply need information and he may be the only person who can give it to me."

"My husband is in poor health. He doesn't need this sort of thing."

"I apologize if I caused any harm, Lilly, but you have to take my word for it. There's a great deal at stake and a number of very important questions need to be answered."

"Like what?"

"I believe that a project your father worked on many years ago has resurfaced with threatening overtones."

"I'm sorry, but I just don't understand."

"It's all right, Lilly." Harry Penn came across the porch and stood beside her. "What Mr. Skyler said didn't upset me. Only the memories he awoke."

"What do you mean?"

"Go in and greet our other guests. Mr. Skyler and I are going to take a walk down to my shop. I'll tell you all about it later."

"Are you sure?"

"Absolutely." He gave her a kiss on the cheek. "Now go."

Reluctantly, Lilly left them and went inside.

Once she was gone, Harry Penn said, "I'm a Catholic, Mr. Skyler, but I haven't been to confession in years. I'm looking forward to this."

THORPE'S CANDLE

Harry Penn sat at his workbench and picked up a colorful trout fly. The inside of his shop was dark except for the soft glow of a lamp over his work area. Skyler heard the gentle lapping of the waves against the old Boston Whaler.

"After we talked this afternoon," Penn said, "I made some calls to a couple of my old friends in Washington. You have quite a reputation as a man of integrity and resources."

Skyler leaned against the bench, shrugging. "I do my job."

"And quite well I might add. You lifted a Soviet nuclear sub off the floor of the Atlantic that defused a potential political disaster. You also discovered six new species of deep-sea marine life under the Arctic, mapped a large chunk of the Amazon River, and discovered a Spanish treasure galleon off the Yucatan Peninsula. I understand it turned out to be the biggest cache of silver in history. I'd say you do your job well."

"I need your help in solving this mystery."

"I don't know if I can solve anything, but I may be able to shed some light on it." Harry Penn took a deep breath. "You know we found it by accident."

"Found what?"

"Candle Power."

"So there was a Project Candle Power?" Skyler asked with a bit of relief.

"At the time, we were working on trying to produce cold fusion. There was a brilliant young physicist on the team who was close to perfecting the right conditions to make it work. We had narrowed our primary element down to palladium. One day he substituted a rare mineral called korium in place of the palladium. What he got was a nuclear reaction—small but impressive. Believe me, it put the fear of God in everyone. He created a whole new category of energy expansion that came close to vaporizing the containment section of the lab. It was only because we had anticipated some violent possibilities and protected ourselves that no one was hurt. We knew we had a potentially lethal weapon that could be mass-produced with a few simple ingredients—mainly heavy water which contains a heavy isotope of hydrogen, and a supply of korium. We argued for days about whether to reveal our findings to the Army. I believed at the time that we should hide what we had found, destroy the records and never tell anyone. Some of the others didn't agree and wanted to tell our Army supervisors. They believed themselves heroes or some such. In the end, I was outvoted."

Penn paused to wipe his forehead. "Once we reported our findings, the Army clamped an airtight lid on the project. We weren't allowed to speak to anyone about anything. Remember this was at the height of the Cold War. The results of the project were so secret, outside of our group, I'll bet there were no more than two-dozen people who knew exactly what we had done. Even the President was never told the whole story."

"What happened to the lab?"

"It was heavily contaminated. The only thing that kept the Army from continuing the experiments was that we only had a small supply of korium to start with, just what was left over from our initial experiments at Niagara Technologies. Dr. Thorpe used that up in the cold fusion test. And because there was no other source of the ore, the Army decided to shut the whole operation down to keep word from getting out to the Russians or Chinese. They dismantled the lab into tiny pieces and dumped it down a twelve-mile-deep well in the Mojave Desert. Army engineers poured what seemed like a million yards of concrete down that hellhole to seal it. But I'll bet you anything that if you go out there right now and dig it up, old Thorpe's Candle, that's what we called it, would still be glowing in the dark."

"Thorpe's Candle?"

"Why, yes, it was named after Dr. William Thorpe. Bill was the scientist I spoke of—a brilliant man."

"Have you kept in touch with him?"

"No. He went off to teach at Chapel Hill in North Carolina. Never saw him again. I held my own, Mr. Skyler, but I was never in Bill Thorpe's league." Penn wiped his forehead again with his handkerchief. "So why all the questions?"

Skyler took a deep breath. "I have reason to believe someone is building a weapon using the volatile nature of korium—what's called a korium device. And for whatever reason, I believe they are going to do whatever it takes to find your missing shipment of ore so they can complete the project."

Penn's mouth formed a silent circle. He leaned back, sighed, and cupped his hands over his face. Then he whispered, "Somehow I always knew this would come back to haunt us. Candle Power could not be hidden forever." He looked at Skyler. "What are you going to do now?"

"I have to find that cargo plane before they do. If whoever is doing this get their hands on it first, we could have a situation that would make the Cuban Missile Crisis look like a friendly game of badminton."

"I wish I could help. I feel somewhat responsible for this mess."

"You have helped. And don't worry, we'll find it. The question is, will we find it first? I've been unable to track down any information through the Internet on the lost cargo flight. I'm starting a search of the old aviation records in London tomorrow. Once I get a general idea of where that plane crashed, OceanQuest has some fascinating technology for locating lost objects. Not only can we find the needle in the haystack, we can tell you what color of thread was used last and probably who's wearing the socks it mended." Skyler turned to leave but stopped. "One more thing."

"Certainly."

"Was your Dr. Thorpe for or against revealing Candle Power?"

"Why for, of course. He was the one that wanted to be a hero."

"He may still get the chance."

SLEEPING BEAUTY

As the last of the Pennsylvania Avenue mercury vapor street lamps faded, the men gathered in the Crisis Command Center deep below the main levels of the White House. There were hushed voices and few smiles, only nods and short greetings.

When everyone had settled around the large conference table, the President said, "Thank you for coming. I want candid analysis, your gut feelings, and honest recommendations. No holding back today, gentlemen."

He searched the faces of the five men and considered the immense power they wielded over so many lives. Under the present circumstances, what they decided today could well affect the future of not only the United States, but also the entire world. The President's eyes fell on Alan Grant, Director of the CIA, who leafed through a spiral notebook. Because the meeting was called on such short notice, Grant still wore his Polo jogging suit.

"Alan, why don't you start?"

"Thank you, Mr. President. This morning, a coded communiqué arrived from our friends in White Hall. It had an Anvil rating so according to protocol I received an immediate call at home. Because of the Anvil classification, I'm required to come in and review it in person—no faxes, e-mail, or text. It was from Sleeping Beauty."

There was a slight reaction as the President realized the message was from the highest levels of the British Secret Service. Anything from "Sleeping Beauty" meant top secret of the gravest urgency. The Agency's code name for the same level of urgency was "Scare Crow".

Grant went on. "An operative working in close proximity to the Communist General Secretary of North Korea overheard a conversation that related to a shipment of Cuban korium. There appears to be no doubt that the North Koreans are involved in developing what they referred to as a korium device."

"Is this operative reliable?" General Mitchell Greer asked. Already in crisp uniform, the weathered face of the Chairman of the Joint Chiefs of Staff reflected a lifetime commitment to professional soldiering.

Grant glanced at his notes but the President knew he didn't need them. The CIA director was renowned for his photographic memory. "Yes, General," Grant said. "We must assume the device is some sort of weapon."

Again, there were slight murmurs as questioning glances shot around the room. Only the President showed no outward reaction. "Go on, Alan."

"I've ordered our science division to come up with an explanation of what a korium device might be. The communiqué contained a reference to an American scientist, a Dr. William Thorpe, who apparently is assisting in the development of this device."

JOE MOORE

"Do you have anything on Thorpe?" Buck Stone said. The Secretary of Defense sipped black coffee and crossed his long Texas legs. Lizard-skin cowboy boots stuck out of his Wrangler jeans. The President had heard Stone carried a small automatic pistol in his boot but no one had ever seen it.

"Yes," Grant said. "I've already run a background check. He's the former head of the physics department at the University of North Carolina, Chapel Hill. Renowned for his work on alternative energy experiments, did some work for the government in the late 1990's. Thorpe moved to Mexico after the death of his wife and worked for a pharmaceutical company for a few years."

"Any idea what he's doing now?" asked Dean Clancy, National Security Adviser. Clancy was a former federal prosecutor, Attorney General of New York, and Ambassador to the UN.

"We have unconfirmed reports that he's working for Pablo Escandoza," Grant said. "It's also believed that Escandoza and his associate, Colonel Felix Blackstone, have recently acquired a former Soviet nuclear missile submarine from the North Koreans."

"Are you serious?" Nathan Templeton, White House Chief of Staff, jerked the stem of the calabash briar pipe from between his teeth. He was not allowed to smoke in the White House, but he always had the pipe with him. "You're telling us that one of the most ruthless men on the planet has the use of a nuclear missile submarine?"

"Holy Mother," Buck Stone said. "Have those fucking Russians lost their minds?"

"Actually," Grant said calmly, "we think the Koreans got the sub from the Ukrainians, But I agree, this goes beyond even Escandoza's usual tricks."

"Tell me about Escandoza," the President said.

106

"Certainly," Grant continued. "Pablo Escandoza rose to power fifteen years ago by systematically assassinating the heads of the other Colombian drug cartels. As Nathan pointed out, he is ruthless, responsible for the deaths of Colombia's Attorney General, a Justice Minister, three Presidential candidates, dozens of journalists, and at least one thousand police officers. And that's just the ones we know about. His personal worth is estimated at three hundred and twenty billion dollars and his business interests are diverse. They include: shipping, banking, real estate holdings around the world, cattle ranches throughout South America, high tech electronics manufacturing and pharmaceuticals in Mexico, dozens of front organizations from Hong Kong to New York, and of course, narcotics. His control over Colombia is solid. Anyone of authority is on his payroll. We'll get little cooperation from the government in conducting any type of investigation to locate Escandoza's operation."

"All right, gentlemen," the President said. "I think it's obvious that we have a serious situation here. I have not been up front in what I already know, so now is the time to take this to the next level." He picked up the phone. "Ask Colonel Argentine to join us."

~ ~ ~

It took just over forty minutes for Argentine to brief the men in the basement command center. When he finished, they sat in stunned silence.

Finally, the President said, "General Greer, give us a status report on the military situation in North Korea."

Greer pulled out a folder from his briefcase. "We have thirty-seven thousand American soldiers stationed in the South. The South Korean army numbers six hundred thirty-three thousand. In opposition, North Korea has the fifth largest army in the world with about one-point-one million soldiers. Add to that half a million reservists and a hundred thousand commandos and you've got a third of their population ready to fight."

The General unfolded a map, laying it on the table. Then he continued, "Hardware wise, the North has twice the battle tanks, eight times the surface-to-surface missiles and almost twice the combat aircraft as the South. They've also got two and a half times the artillery along with short- and medium-range missiles capable of carrying nuclear warheads. About seventy percent of the active-duty forces are stationed within sixty miles from the DMZ, which is only thirty-five miles from Seoul. As you know, Seoul is a primary target with eleven million people and a heavy concentration of industry. The North has massed most of its four thousand, five hundred self-propelled guns and two thousand mobile rocket launchers within firing range of Seoul." He paused, taking a sip of water before continuing.

"We're all familiar with their regular missile- and nuclear tests. In the event of an attack on the South, the Pentagon's Office of Net Assessment predicts that the defensive lines set up by the South would be quickly breached by North Korean artillery. If that happened, the North could probably take the whole of the South in a week or two. Of course, this is based on a conventional assessment. Up until now, we had no knowledge of anything like this device described by Colonel Argentine. If the korium weapon becomes a reality, then all our projections are nil."

"Further assessments, gentlemen?" the President said.

"Do we have a carrier group in the region?" Nathan Templeton asked.

Greer nodded. "The *Nimitz* is off the coast of southern Japan. She could be in position within twenty-four hours."

"Then I suggest we rattle some sabers," Templeton said as he tapped the stem of his pipe on the table top. "Move the *Nimitz* and her support group off the North Korean coast."

"And find that damn submarine," Stone added.

"How hard would that be, General?" the President asked.

"I'm not an expert on naval tactics, Mr. President," Greer said, "But I did confer with my colleagues at the Pentagon before coming here. Apparently, the best way to find a submarine is with another submarine. That's because the ability of a submarine to hide is defined almost entirely by its environment—the temperature of the water, salinity variations, the placement of thermal layers, and of course, ambient noise. Aircraft and surface ships can see bits and pieces of what lies below, but the submarine commander has a great deal more latitude in assessing his environment and his best hiding places.

"Each class of sub has its own distinctive ambient signature, and for that matter, each individual sub does as well. I've been assured that we know the Yankee-class intimately having tracked them for decades. By today's standards, they're old and clunky—fairly easy to find. Their own acoustic signature is their worst enemy. We can assume that the sub in question is somewhere off the west coast of Central or South America which would narrow the search field down considerably. I feel certain that we can locate her within a matter of days."

"And what about the korium?" Stone asked.

Alan Grant answered, "The British communiqué said the Koreans and Escandoza have found another source. Colonel Argentine, do you have any idea what that might be?"

"We scanned virtually every square mile of land where any trace of korium was ever known to have been found. At this time, we know of no other supply."

"But the British communiqué mentioned that Escandoza had a lead," Stone pressed. "Any guess as to what they were talking about?"

"No, Mr. Secretary," Argentine said. "Believe me, when we discovered Project Candle Power and the importance of korium in developing Thorpe's Candle, we followed every possible lead we could think of to find a new source. The Cuban mine was all we could come up with."

The President said, "We have to find that korium before the Koreans do. I want you to begin a new search immediately."

"Yes, sir," Argentine said.

"What was the name of that outfit that lifted the Soviet sub, Colonel?"

"OceanQuest, sir."

"Get them involved."

"Alan," the President continued, nodding to Grant, "do we have any idea where Escandoza's headquarters is located?"

"We believe it is somewhere in the Andes Mountains near Lake Guatavita."

"But you don't feel we would get any cooperation from the Colombian authorities?"

"No, Mr. President, none whatsoever."

"All right. I want an extensive satellite scan of the suspected area. At the same time, assemble a strike force and put together a plan of action to be carried out when we do find him. I've already briefed the Director of the FBI on the situation and have him searching on how the Koreans found out about Project Candle Power in the first place.

And I want to know how the Cubans knew Captain Harper was coming down there. Remember that if word of the korium device leaks out, the effect on world stability would be devastating. Everything must be at the highest level of security."

Each man nodded as the President said, "The race is on, gentlemen. Coming in second is not an option."

SMYTH

"I was thirty-two when that plane went down, Mr. Skyler, but I still remember it. Lost without a trace." The gray-haired woman thumbed through the library-style drawers filled with index cards.

"So you'll have the records of the search attempts?"

"Oh, my, yes. We keep everything."

Skyler wondered with today's technology how an arm of the British government could be so antiquated in its record-keeping procedures. He patiently watched from behind the massive counter stretching across the room on the third floor of the Royal Aviation and Marine Archives building. Located on Leadenhall Street near Lloyd's of London, the building had stood since 1881.

Skyler had fond memories of London, having spent three months doing research on eighteenth century British shipwrecks during the summer of his junior year. His flat had been on top of an Edwardian house looking south from Hampstead down over central London. At night, when the wind blew and the low clouds rolled past his window, he sometimes sat for hours staring at the city—St.

Paul's Cathedral, Big Ben and the spires of Westminster. And in the mornings before going to the archives, he would stand on the Embankment and watch the River Thames move slowly past carrying with it the dust of ages. Skyler was glad to be back in London as he watched the old woman examining the reference cards.

"Here it is, Mr. Skyler." She held up a card in a victory gesture. "Give me a moment and I'll have your files." With a warm smile, she made her way past the card catalog file cabinets and disappeared into the cavernous records vault.

"Thanks, Gertrude," Skyler said when she returned a few minutes later carrying a brown accordion folder. He took the bundle and went to one of the many long tables set up for researchers and investigators. The folder was fairly heavy, and as he untied the string that held it together, he expected to find reports from the Royal Air Force Search and Rescue, the Icelandic Coast Guard or Newfoundland's Civil Air and Search organization. What he found instead was a full ream of blank white paper. All the records of the search for Arctic Air Cargo 101 were gone.

"That was quick," Gertrude said, looking up.

Skyler set the folder down on the counter. "Gertrude, do you have a record of the individuals who checked out this file before me?"

"Oh, yes, regulations you know." She noted the reference number on the file folder and then searched through her sign-out logs. After five minutes of obvious frustration, she turned to Skyler. "I just don't understand. There's got to be a record, it's the rules. But there's nothing here. Someone's misplaced it. I just don't understand."

"Yes, I'm sure, Gertrude," Skyler said with a half-smile

"I know it's here somewhere."

As she continued her fruitless exercise, Matt Skyler turned and walked away already knowing that she could search forever—there would be no log. Without those reports he faced a dead end.

~~~

Skyler decided rather than take a taxi back to Knightsbridge Green, the Georgian hotel across from Hyde Park where he was staying, he would drop into the Woolpack, a smoky little pub he visited many years ago on his first trip to London. The financial district was closing and the sidewalks were crowded with office workers, stockbrokers, tourists, and bankers heading home. Strolling along Finch Lane, he got the feeling he was being followed, but a look over his shoulder from time to time revealed only the disinterested faces of those whose thoughts seemed miles away.

Young men and women who worked in the London Stock Exchange packed the bar. Laughing and joking, they were obviously glad to have finished the day. Skyler made his way through the crowd and slipped into a small booth near the back. A young girl with long red hair and freckles asked for his order.

"Guinness," he said with a smile.

"Make that two." The man slipped into the booth opposite Skyler. He appeared short and overweight with a balding head, thick glasses, and a double chin. He winked at the waitress. "I believe it's my turn to buy Mr. Skyler a drink." The stranger placed a briefcase on the seat beside him.

Skyler remembered seeing the man on the street, but his rumpled, ill-fitted appearance didn't hint at unusual at the time. A mistake, he thought. The two men eyed each other as the waitress walked away. Then Skyler said, "I don't recall buying the last round, friend. Mind refreshing my memory?"

"Relax. You're in no danger. I'm here to get a little information." He extended a meaty hand across the table holding a laminated plastic ID card in front of Skyler. "Walter Smyth, Chief Inspector, Gordan Insurance Company."

The redhead returned with the two pints, smiled at Skyler and left.

"Okay, Mr. Smyth," Skyler said. "You've got my attention. What do you want?"

"Why are you looking for the lost Arctic Air Cargo plane?"

"I run a salvage company. I've been contracted by the insurer to locate and recover it."

"That's interesting, Mr. Skyler, since Gordan is the insurer. I'd say you were a liar."

Skyler shrugged, aggravated that his quick thinking wasn't quick enough. "Guilty as charged. But first tell me why you want to know?"

"Two reasons. Number one—it's my job. Like I said, I work for an insurance company—we underwrite financial institutions. When a bank gets robbed or someone embezzles funds, I try to recover the money so Gordan Insurance doesn't have to pay." He took a sip of his Guinness. "That's why I'm here."

"Why the interest after all these years? The claim couldn't have been that much."

"For the plane, no. But it's more than the loss of an old cargo plane. You see, back in 1961, a branch of Barclays was held up. The thieves got away with one and a half-million pounds. It took Scotland Yard over two years to round up the three men who pulled the heist. Funny thing. When the crooks were finally caught, they swore they only stole a million pounds. There was another half-million missing. Re-opening the investigation revealed that during the robbery, the bad guys locked two people in the vault— they were trapped overnight due to the time lock. One was a teller who was so traumatized that she died of a heart attack before they got her out. The other was a bank customer. Naturally the Yard wanted to know what happened to the rest of the money. When they went to question the customer, a fellow by the name of Henry Bristol, they discovered that he had died in a fire at his flat a short time after the robbery. Checking the official report, they found that arson was the cause of the fire—a blaze so intense, Bristol's remains could not be positively identified. But the general features—height and weight of the body— were identical. So the authorities assumed it was him. The police report also stated that witnesses saw Bristol on the night of the fire in the company of a local homeless vagrant. Next thing you know, the house burns down, they find a body that resembles Bristol, and for lack of any further evidence, the case fades away."

"I assume that Gordan insured the stolen bank loot?" Skyler asked.

"Yes."

"I still don't get the connection between Bristol and the plane."

"We also insured Arctic Air Cargo. When the plane went down, the investigation revealed that a nervous little man matching Bristol's description showed up at Arctic Air's office and bribed the pilot of flight 101 to take him to Canada. I'm convinced that man was Henry Bristol. When he walked out of that vault, police reports stated he carried a duffel bag full of dirty clothes—he told them he was on his way to the laundry when he stopped by the bank to cash his paycheck. Nobody bothered to check it because they assumed *he* was the victim. Later, they found some old clothes stuffed in the bottom of a bunch of money pouches in the vault. I think Henry Bristol saw his chance to steal a bag full of money and I believe he was willing to kill for it.

He was using flight 101 to flee the country when it disappeared. Really bad luck. My job is to prove it and get the money back. When I heard you were asking about the cargo plane, I ran a background check tracing you to London."

"If Bristol was on that plane, who died in the fire?"

"I think it was the homeless vagrant, a fellow by the name of Lenny Smyth."

"Any relation?"

"That's the second reason I'm here, Mr. Skyler. Lenny Smyth was my father. I want to put a proper headstone on his grave and get to the bottom of what really happened to him. Despite what my mother told me for years, I always believed he was a good man and didn't run out on us. So I've got to find that plane and recover the half-million. It's the proof I need to put this whole affair to rest."

"There's a problem," Skyler said. "Someone's taken the file on 101 from the archives. At this point, I have no idea where the plane crashed or where to start the search."

"That means someone else is interested, too." Smyth glanced suspiciously around the room. "Now I've told you my story. It's your turn. Why are you looking for the plane?"

"Do you remember what the cargo was?"

"Ore. Insured for twenty thousand pounds."

"There's your answer, my friend. Let's just say that the ore has appreciated in value."

Smyth opened his briefcase and rummaged through a file. He pulled out a sheet of paper. "Korium," he said, reading. "Mined from a small site in Iceland, ordered and shipped to a plating company in Buffalo, New York. So it's increased in value enough to interest an organization like OceanQuest?"

"And then some."

"The search for 101 lasted two weeks. There was no trace of the wreckage. What makes you think you can do any better?"

"Trust me, Chief Inspector. Technology has come a long way since 1961. We'll find her."

"You do come with some impressive credentials. If you say the ore is the reason you're snooping around, I believe you. That's why I'm going to extend an offer that will make your life a lot easier." He opened his briefcase again, taking out a bulging folder. "A complete photocopy of the archive search file on Arctic Air. I made it years ago."

"And the price?" Skyler asked with apprehension.

"A simple request. In return for the file, I want to be there when you find 101. I want to know first-hand that it was Bristol. Then I can sleep a little easier at night. What do you say?"

Skyler scanned the faces in the crowded bar and looked at the fat little man with the thick fingers and bald head. "I hope you've got a good warm coat, Mr. Smyth." He reached for the file. "It's pretty chilly in the North Atlantic, even in the dead of summer."

SHOOTING STAR

The Pacific Ocean west of Cedros Island, Mexico

The black ocean moved in apprehensive swells somehow knowing the huge object was there. A tense breeze swept away the clouds exposing a clear, starry night. Even the fiercest predators turned away, diving deep into the protective depths as the leviathan maneuvered into position. On its back, the titanium door that shielded its deadly cargo opened like a slow-motion jack-in-the-box revealing the cone-shaped nose of the SS-N-17 "Snipe" ballistic missile.

Inside the *Mako Shark*, the fire-control officer pressed a series of buttons on an elaborate, semicircular electronics console. His actions initiated the launch sequence as he spoke the target coordinates into his headset microphone.

A crewman in the missile bay listened to the numbers. He then reached his arm through a small opening until his fingers touched a numeric keypad inside ballistic missile number three. He punched in the coordinates and watched the numbers appear on a red digital readout above his hand.

Reading them back for confirmation, he then closed and sealed the access doors on the outside of the missile and finally closed the small, thick door on the missile tube. Yanking his headphone connector from its socket, he raced along the catwalk that ran beside the other SLBM tubes and jumped through the hatch into the launch support compartment. Two of his fellow crewmen slammed the emergency blast door shut and spun the wheel, sealing it tight.

The fire-control officer then pressed another series of buttons and reached inside his shirt to remove a key that hung on a chain around his neck. He inserted it into a lock on the console. A second man, standing just out of arms-length, took a key from around his neck and inserted it into a lock on the console.

"On my mark," The fire-control officer nodded to the second man. "Three—two—one."

With a click, the two men rotated their keys from the "unarmed" position 45 degrees straight up to the "armed" position. The section of the control panel designating missile warhead status shifted from blue to blood red.

"Missile armed, Colonel," the fire-control officer said. His hand gripped what looked like a video game joystick—his finger on the trigger. With temples pounding and sweat beading on his forehead, he stared at the digital displays.

A few seconds later, a voice came through his headset. "Fire-control, this is Colonel Blackstone. Fire your missile."

His hand tightened on the joystick, and he squeezed the trigger.

RUSTY ROCKETS

"**B**ut the point is, Senator," General Westfield said, "cutting back on the weapons we need to defend this country is insane."

Westfield and Tennessee Senator Harlin Davis were alone in the glass-enclosed VIP observation booth. They overlooked the command center of Space Defense Operations deep inside Cheyenne Mountain, Colorado.

"General, the cold war is long gone, nothing more than a chapter in the history books. There's no need to maintain this elaborate level of surveillance. Do you really think anybody is going to shoot a ballistic missile at us?"

Davis was the budget-cutting chairman of the Senate Armed Services Committee. He smiled his famous toothy smile. "The Russians? The Koreans? The Chinese? They're all bankrupt. They can't even afford to pay the salaries of the men that would launch their rusty old rockets." Davis made a sweeping gesture. "No, General, this is an obsolete—" He stopped when he realized the general was no longer listening.

Westfield had turned to watch the sudden increase in activity below. Dozens of Air Force weapons detection and tracking specialists manned rows of computer banks stretching across what resembled an indoor amphitheater. Normally, they monitored redundant scanning and sensing programs along with traffic and telemetry analysis, and satellite communications. They also kept track of activity and anomalies in the lower and upper atmosphere. But as Westfield watched, a number of operators stood and pointed at the large video display dominating the front wall. It showed different regions of the world with emphasis on Southeast Asia, Afghanistan, the Middle East, the Mediterranean, and parts of China and the former Soviet Union. A few technicians moved over to stand behind a young staff sergeant who was programming confirmation sequences into her computer terminal.

"Senator, will you excuse me for a moment?" Westfield turned to leave.

"What's going on, General? Another one of your wasteful, expensive war games?"

Rather than stay in the observation booth, Davis followed Westfield along a hallway and down a flight of stairs. At the bottom, a military policeman opened a door for the general but held his hand up to halt Davis.

"Son," Davis said as he rose up to his full height, "are you detaining a United States Senator from conducting his duty to his constituents?"

Westfield called over his shoulder, "It's all right, Sergeant." He waited for Davis to catch up and they moved over to the group of technicians gathered around the staff sergeant. As Westfield and Davis approached, a path cleared for them.

The duty officer, Lt. Col. Patricia Beck, stood behind the technician. She turned to Westfield. "We have a launch detect, General. Our Pacific listening stations have confirmed a thermal bloom."

"Can you plot it?" Westfield asked.

"Give me ten more seconds, sir." Beck turned to face the huge, panoramic projection screen. "Here it comes now."

All eyes watched as a small black triangle appeared off the coast of Mexico and started a slow, creeping path out over the Pacific. A series of numbers appeared under the object as telemetry data updated.

"Is it one of ours?" Westfield asked.

"No. It has the signature and footprint of an SS-N-17, sir." Beck never took her eyes off the triangle. "We have booster stage separation."

"This is most impressive," Davis said with a smile. "You boys like to make things realistic. I have to admit that for a moment I thought somebody had really launched a missile."

"What's the target," Westfield said as he ignored the senator.

"Too soon, sir." Beck read the numbers appearing on the screen, then calmly said, "Altitude twenty-three miles and climbing."

Westfield picked up a phone, pressing the direct line to the National Military Command Center in the Pentagon. He looked up at the DEFCON (Defense Configurations) status on the screen. Level four, a condition he had taken for granted for years, changed automatically to three, a state of military alert activated by the launch of any ICBM. He knew that if it went to level two, it meant an impending attack. And level one would mean a state of nuclear war existed.

He looked at Davis. With an edge to his voice that caused everyone around him to turn and stare, he said, "So much for your rusty rockets theory, Senator."

CANDLE LIGHT

It was after 8:00 p.m. when Matt Skyler and Walter Smyth walked out of the Woolpack and stood on the London sidewalk. "It's been an interesting evening, Inspector," Skyler said. "Next time it's my turn to buy."

"Just find that plane and the rounds will always be on me, my friend."

"Deal." Skyler realized he liked this pudgy little fellow with the balding head. He smiled and they shook hands, the file of search records securely under Skyler's arm.

Suddenly, Smyth turned and stared into the window of an electronics store next to the pub. A dozen TV's all blinked back at him, their screens covered with the flashing message: A CNN SPECIAL BULLETIN. MYSTERY DETONATION OVER HAWAII. As the anchorperson appeared with a map of Hawaii above her left shoulder, Skyler and Smyth stepped into the store to hear the audio.

"*A mysterious explosion lit up the sky over the state of Hawaii early this morning, causing widespread panic and fueling speculation that a satellite, a rocket or possibly some sort of space craft blew up in the upper atmosphere. Witnesses described a light brighter than the noonday sun appeared at 5:47 a.m. local time. It lasted for approximately twenty seconds before slowly fading to a pinpoint of high intensity light and then disappearing altogether. A spokesperson for the Air Force said the source of the light was as yet unknown but a full-scale investigation would soon be underway. We go now to Honolulu for the latest developments."*

"Isn't that the strangest thing," Smyth said as he turned to Skyler.

But the director of OceanQuest was already out of the store, running at a full sprint with his cell phone pressed to his ear.

BELTWAY AMBUSH

Washington, DC

The British Airways 777 touched down at Dulles twenty-six miles west of Washington. It was two minutes past midnight. Watching the runway lights race by, Skyler mulled over the details of the explosion in the sky over Hawaii. A phone call from Heathrow to Gates had confirmed the detonation of an unknown device in the outer fringes of the atmosphere. Gates also relayed an urgent message from a Colonel Michael Argentine summoning them both to Washington. There was no doubt about it now, Skyler realized—someone had constructed Thorpe's Candle.

Gates had verified through his government sources that a submarine missile launch took place. Bets were it was from the pirate sub Skyler had seen running alongside the Aztec Princess. Skyler and Gates debated if it was a show of force, an attack that went south, or some kind of accident. Had someone already found the lost shipment of korium in Greenland and started producing Candles?

A chime brought Skyler out of deep thought—it sounded when the captain turned off the "fasten seat belts sign" as the plane parked at the terminal. Skyler pulled his carryall from the overhead bin and followed the slow procession of passengers up the entrance tunnel. When he emerged into the gate area, two men wearing dark suits and serious expressions approached. The first was a bull of a man well over six and a half feet tall with thick hands and a shaved head. The second was about Skyler's height, slim with a round face, short hair, and a thin mustache.

"Mr. Skyler," the first man said. "Special Agent Daniel Tyson, FBI." He extended his credentials for Skyler to examine. "This is Agent Knowles. We're here to escort you to your destination."

"Which is?" Skyler asked.

Tyson motioned. "This way please."

The trio moved away from the gate area to U.S. Customs and Immigration. At the inspection point, Tyson showed his credentials and Skyler was ushered through the gates into baggage claim. He had not checked any bags so the three men were able to walk out to the street where a Ford Explorer waited at curbside. An airport security officer stood guard.

Skyler sat in the back, the two agents up front. They pulled away from the curb, heading east toward the Capital Beltway. "Where are we going?" Skyler asked after a few minutes of silence.

Agent Knowles glanced at Skyler from the rear view mirror as he guided the Explorer south among the sparse Interstate traffic toward Arlington Boulevard. "Important people want the pleasure of your company, Mr. Skyler."

"Can you tell me if Mickey Gates has arrived yet?"

"I believe he is still in route," Tyson said as the sleepy communities and empty mall parking lots glided by.

Fatigued, and in need of a shower and change of clothes, Skyler started to lose patience. He was about to say so when he realized Knowles was watching the rear view mirror more than the highway ahead. "Is there something wrong?"

Knowles motioned with his head and Tyson turned, staring into the glare of the headlights behind them.

"Probably nothing," Tyson said.

"They've been with us since we left Dulles," Knowles said. "I think we've got uninvited guests."

"Speed up," Tyson said. "Let's see what they do."

Skyler stole a glance over his shoulder and saw a set of headlights pacing the Explorer about five car lengths back.

Tyson pulled a cellular phone from his pocket. "We're on the Capital Beltway heading south near exit 11. Looks like we've picked up a tail." He listened for a moment then disconnected. "Virginia State police are on the way." Just as he nodded to Knowles the back window shattered.

The Explorer swerved, the tires squealed, and Skyler was thrown forward. His head banged against the back of the seat. As he pulled himself up, Knowles yelled, "Dan's hit."

Dazed, Skyler looked over the seat and strained to focus on the slumped-over body of Agent Tyson. Blood flowed from wounds on the back of his head and neck. Skyler located the man's weapon—a Browning 9mm automatic. He pulled back the bolt as a second burst of gunfire slammed into the trunk and fender of the Explorer.

"Get us out of here!" Skyler yelled and aimed over the back seat. He fired three shots at the headlights. The chase vehicle swerved, momentarily losing speed.

The Explorer roared as Knowles floored the accelerator, making large evasive sweeps back and forth across the three lanes of the Interstate. Skyler looked at the glow of the dashboard—the speedometer pointed at one hundred.

A third barrage of bullets tore into the Explorer, this time turning the shatterproof windshield into a mass of spider-webbed cracks. Large chunks of glass separated allowing the one hundred mile-per-hour wind to blast into the car. Knowles screamed, trying to cover his face as tiny pieces of glass peppered him. The Explorer careened across the highway. It skidded over the shoulder, down an embankment and into a stand of small evergreens lining the road. The car crashed into a fence and spun around facing the opposite direction. It dug a path through the dirt and trees. The sound of breaking wood and scraping metal assaulted Skyler's ears.

No sooner had the Explorer come to rest than he heard the screech of brakes—the pursuers stopping beside the highway a hundred feet away. Skyler scrambled out through the back window and tumbled to the ground.

Knowles was slumped over the front seat, moaning.

"Hang on, buddy," Skyler said as he gripped the passenger's door. Jammed! He put his foot on the side of the car and pulled the handle. With a groan, the door gave way. He dragged Tyson and Agent Knowles out of the car onto the ground. Then he turned his attention back to the highway.

There was a plain white panel van silhouetted in the lights of the Interstate. Two figures moved down the crest of the embankment. Skyler saw the glint of light reflecting on their guns. He took aim and fired. The two men opened fire and raked the Explorer with automatic spray.

Skyler waited behind the fender until the barrage stopped for an instant. Then he rose, took quick aim and fired again. Both men retreated at the sound of an approaching siren. The van shot onto the Beltway leaving a spray of gravel and dirt behind. Skyler turned his attention to the two agents. Tyson was lifeless but Knowles groaned with pain. Brakes squealed from the direction of the highway and the LEDs of the trooper's car washed the surroundings with alternating red and blue. Skyler heard the metallic voices from the police radio as the trooper moved down the embankment, a gun aimed at the demolished Ford Explorer.

"Let me see your hands!" the trooper yelled and worked his way around the back of the agent's car.

A wail of sirens filled the air as Skyler felt blood flowing down his own face—the sting from glass fragments in his scalp swept over him like a swarm of bees. Dizzy and weak, he dropped the Browning and raised his hands.

"Don't shoot," he managed to mumble as he looked into the barrel of the trooper's automatic.

OVAL OFFICE

A female intern at the George Washington University Hospital emergency room cleaned and stitched the lacerations on Skyler's head. One was at the edge of his hairline and two on his scalp. A fourth across his left arm had been swabbed and butterflied. Skyler watched the steady parade of victims, the result he was told by the intern, of random shootings, car crashes, house fires, drug overdoses, rapes, and muggings. An army of medical emergency and trauma specialists attended to all—a typical Saturday night in the inner city.

While the intern worked on him, Skyler was surrounded by law enforcement officers—D.C. detectives and city police, FBI agents, ATF agents, State Police, and a number of men in suits who never bothered to identify their organizations.

He had learned soon after arriving by ambulance that Agent Daniel Tyson had died at the scene. Agent Knowles was in emergency surgery—he had lost his left eye but was expected to recover. The white van had somehow eluded police and disappeared into the Virginia suburbs.

"That should do," the doctor said and snipped the last of the sutures.

"Thanks." Skyler looked down at his dirty, bloodstained clothes. "Wouldn't happen to have a spare outfit I could borrow?"

"Only if you love pale green and don't mind a breeze from the rear." With a weary expression, she moved to a patient in the next partition.

"Mr. Skyler, I'm Colonel Michael Argentine."

Skyler looked up. "Hello, Colonel. Friendly town you got here."

They shook hands. "We usually don't start shooting visitors until they're *inside* the Beltway. But for important people like you, we make exceptions."

"Don't do me any favors." Skyler strained a smile. "Any idea who they were?"

"A few theories, probably the same as yours."

"I'll lay odds it was some friends of mine from south of the border."

"Sounds like a sure bet. I didn't realize until a few days ago that it was you who filed the report with the Mexican authorities about the submarine sighting." He lowered his voice. "You've had a first-hand look at Escandoza's latest smuggling techniques and his sub. If I were him, I wouldn't want you around either. He's obviously not as good as he thinks. You're still with us."

"Only means he'll try harder next time."

Over the clamor of the emergency room came a deep booming voice. "Sky, I can't leave you alone for one moment without you getting into trouble."

Skyler and Argentine turned to see Mickey Gates push his way through the crowd. A detective held out an arm to stop the burly military salvage expert, but Argentine said, "He's cleared," and motioned Gates through.

Gates leaned in to take a closer look at the shaved portions of Skyler's head and the stitches. Then he extended his hand to the Colonel. "So you must be our mystery date."

"Afraid so," Argentine said, and they shook hands.

"Well, Colonel," Skyler said, "you called this meeting. Now how about some answers."

"Gentlemen, all your answers will come soon. First we need to take a ride."

"That's how my troubles started in the first place." Skyler eased off the examination table.

"This time, we're going to give you a little more protection." A contingency of law enforcement officers surrounded Skyler, Gates and Argentine, and moved them out the emergency exit to a line of waiting police cars and motorcycles.

"If this is the treatment we get," Gates said as they approached a black Chevrolet Suburban with dark tinted windows, "I'd like to see what you guys do for the President."

"The President doesn't make a lot of visits to the GWTC emergency room." Argentine held the door open for the two men.

After leaving the underground entrance, the entourage split into three groups. A few moments later, there were only the Suburban and two black & whites, one leading and one following. They moved through the downtown streets of the nation's capital with ease, the lead car remotely triggering the traffic lights to green in time for the caravan to pass through the intersections.

Changing into fresh clothes from his recovery carryall, Skyler watched as they weaved in and out of the light, 4:00 a.m. traffic. He soon saw familiar landmarks—the Capitol, the Washington Monument, and the White

House. Within seconds they were cleared through the Northwest Gate. Before Skyler could take in the immense grandeur of his surroundings, he and Gates along with Argentine were ushered into the building and down a series of hallways, and finally into the Oval Office.

Three men sat on the couches positioned on the carpet that bore the crest of the President of the United States. Skyler recognized Alan Grant, Director of the CIA, Dean Clancy, National Security Adviser, and Thomas Lancaster, Secretary of the Navy.

"Come in, gentlemen," Dean Clancy said. "Please be seated. Can we get you something to drink?"

"Diet Coke," Argentine said.

"Coffee, black," Skyler requested.

"A beer, if you got one." Gates took a seat at the end of one couch, leaned back, and crossed his arms over his chest.

"I'm sure we can find you a beer, Mr. Gates." Clancy shot him a condescending smile. "Please, Mr. Skyler, make yourself at home. You too, Colonel."

Skyler sat beside Gates while Argentine took a vacant spot on a couch across from the two.

"We're waiting for a few late arrivals," Clancy said, "then we can get started."

Just then the door opened. Everyone including Skyler and Gates turned and stood as the President entered the room. Two other men followed him.

"Sorry I'm late." The President approached with his hand extended. "Gentlemen, thank you for coming on such short notice. I'd like you to meet Dr. John Dolen, Managing Director of Deep Scan, and Professor Carl Reynolds, his associate and Deep Scan's Chief of Vital Research."

Skyler and Gates greeted the two scientists while the rest of the group took their seats. The President nodded to the other men before taking his place at his desk. "Well," he said, stretching his arms and interlacing his fingers, "we have a big problem on our hands." He looked at CIA Director Grant. "Alan."

Grant opened a file on the table, taking one quick glance around the room at each individual. "The missile was a Soviet-built SS-N-17, launched from a submarine approximately eight hundred miles west of Cedros Island, off the Mexican coast. Immediately after launching her bird, the sub turned south and disappeared. The missile ran its full range of three thousand nine hundred kilometers skipping across the outer atmosphere, detonating four hundred eighty-two kilometers or three hundred miles above the big island of Hawaii."

"Was this some kind of an attack?" the President asked.

"We don't think so," Grant said. "There was never any telemetry that would suggest an attempt at re-entry."

"What about any damage to the atmosphere?"

"So far, Mr. President, our sensors indicate minimal disturbances," Grand answered.

"So it was an accident?" Clancy asked.

"Again, probably not," Grant said. "The sub's maneuvers were calculated. We believe this was a deliberate missile launch and detonation. And we think it was intended as a show of force, either to impress us and our allies, or someone else."

"Who might that be, Dean?"

"Based on additional information, Mr. President, from our British colleagues and their operative in North Korea, we think it might be potential customers for the Candles."

"You mean terrorist organizations," Skyler said as the drinks were served.

"Exactly, Mr. Skyler," Grant said. "Anyone looking to jump into the major league weapons business."

"This looks like a sales demonstration to me," Skyler added. "Escandoza must be bored with selling cocaine. Weapons of mass destruction are more glamorous."

Grant said, "I agree. He's formed a partnership with the Koreans to produce and sell korium devices. Because of the loss of the Cuban korium shipment, we think his potential customers were getting cold feet."

"They needed some hand holding," Gates added and sipped his beer. "So they popped off a Candle to assure everyone the merchandise is for real."

"Right, Mr. Gates," Grant said. "We also believe Escandoza is going to attempt to assemble the weapons at a new location somewhere in Colombia. We've tracked a number of suspicious transport planes leapfrogging across the Pacific from Pyongyang to Bogota for the past three days."

"Who's operating that sub, Alan?" the President said.

"The man in charge is ex-Soviet naval officer, Colonel Felix Blackstone. After the fall of the Soviet Union, he became a commando in the elite Black Knights of the Belgium Army. He served three years in a military prison for attempted rape. A year after his release, he surfaced as a major player in the Eastern European black market. He progressed into selling weapons, became a mercenary and finally graduated summa cum terrorist. Spent time in Italy working for the Red Brigade, and from there he moved on to Colombia to become Escandoza's right arm. He's carried out a number of assassinations for the drug lord and has vowed never to be taken alive. There's no telling how many men Blackstone has killed. In summary, gentlemen, he is to be considered extremely dangerous and unpredictable."

"How does a man like Blackstone put together a crew for a nuclear submarine?" the President asked.

"Easier than you might think, sir," Grand said. "The Russian Navy suffered severely for years after the collapse of the Soviet Union—insufficient maintenance, lack of funding and subsequent effects on the training of personnel, and replacement of outdated equipment. Another setback is because of Russia's domestic shipbuilding industry which has been in decline. There are scores of sailors that served as submariners. Now they can't get a job for which they were trained. All Blackstone needs is one hundred and twenty to man a Yankee-class boomer. My guess is he has an abundance of recruits lining up to come on board for the right price."

The President was silent for a moment, appearing to be deep in thought. Then he turned to the National Security Adviser. "Recommendations, Dean?"

"Mr. President, our actions to stop this madness must be swift and severe. Our first goal is to locate and capture or destroy that pirate sub. We need to have the Navy concentrate all its resources in the Pacific where the sub is projected to be heading."

The President turned to Thomas Lancaster. "You have my authority to use deadly force if necessary. Is that understood?"

The Secretary of the Navy nodded.

Dean Clancy asked, "Alan, any progress on your satellite surveillance search for Escandoza's headquarters?"

"Based on activity over the last few days, we have what we feel are a half-dozen possible sites," Grant said. "An Army Ranger rapid response team is rehearsing in the mountains outside El Centro, California, right now for an assault once we confirm the location."

"Excellent," Clancy said. Then he turned to Skyler. "We also need your help, Mr. Skyler. It is essential that we locate and recover what we think is the only known supply of korium left in the world—the Arctic Air shipment lost in Greenland—and we have to do it before Escandoza gets there. I believe you were investigating its whereabouts while you were in London?"

Skyler nodded.

"As I'm sure you're aware," Clancy continued, "this country is under extreme budget restraints resulting in major cutbacks in our military. We do not have the resources to conduct scientific and research missions. Furthermore, we're required by law to utilize the private sector for any endeavors of this type."

"To make matters worse," the President said, "Greenland is an autonomous territory under the protection of the Kingdom of Denmark."

"I guess they still haven't gotten over the Air Force managing to accidentally drop that cruise missile into downtown Copenhagen," Mickey Gates said.

"Or crashing a B-1b a week later into the Central Government complex in Godthab," Skyler added.

"Exactly," the President said.

"We don't have the time to go through all the proper diplomatic channels and get the appropriate permissions," Clancy said.

"And that's assuming that Denmark or Greenland would agree to any kind of military intrusion of their respective sovereignty or interests," the President added.

"That's why we've brought you and Mr. Gates here," Clancy said. "We need a well-respected salvage organization like OceanQuest to put together the expedition to

Greenland. Working in the background with a number of research groups and universities, we can help push through the appropriate paperwork and get your clearances. In addition, we can supply you critical intelligence support needed to locate and recover the korium shipment."

"But we can't send in the troops," the President said. "To do so would take months of diplomatic wrangling—time we just don't have. Can you do it?"

Skyler said, "Our research ship, *Phoenix*, is currently taking on supplies at Woods Hole Oceanographic Institution on Cape Cod. She was scheduled to begin a search for a Civil War ironclad off the Virginia coast. We can have her and an expedition team ready and assembled in five days." He looked at Gates.

"That's really pushing it, Sky."

"We'll make it happen, Mr. President," Skyler said.

"Good." The President turned to Dr. John Dolen. "Any progress on how the national security files were compromised?"

"Yes, sir," Dolen said, his eyes magnified through the thick lenses of his glasses.

"And we know who did it," Professor Reynolds added, his chubby fingers pulling at the ends of his bushy mustache. "Working with specialists from the FBI, we cross-checked the age of all passwords used in the last twelve months—one had not been used in two decades but had somehow been protected from deletion after the normal dormant usage period. It belonged to Dr. William Thorpe. Thorpe got in and stole the files. Interestingly enough, at the time he did it, there was a major system crash. Part of one of the files he was reading—what became a lost cluster—was thrown across the server's hard drive. Thorpe got back in, finishing his download but he had no way of knowing about the lost cluster. That's the one we found when we discovered Project Candle Power."

"So," the President stated, "Dr. Thorpe is alive and well and working for Escandoza."

Dolen added, "Yes, sir. But it gets worse. We now know he's been in and out of the system many times over the years and we assume he knows about Deep Scan. Until the FBI started investigating and plugged the hole, Thorpe had a wide-open back door to our files. It had to have been him that alerted Escandoza and subsequently the Cubans to Captain Harper and the Rangers."

"Looks like you can add treason to the list of charges when you catch him," Skyler said.

"You can count on it, Mr. Skyler. And now, gentlemen, let's waste no more time here. I wish you all good luck." As he rose, the President said, "Mr. Skyler, we're counting on you to find that plane and the lost shipment of korium."

"Oh, we'll find it, sir." Skyler's expression was stern. "But Escandoza is a determined man. If he gets there first, all that may be left is an empty hole in the ice."

CIRRUS

The North Atlantic

"See anything yet, Boomer?"

The voice came over his headset as the tail-boom operator of the specially modified KC-135Q searched the inky black void. Only a half-hour earlier, he'd watched the sun drop below the horizon and the sky shift from rose to indigo. Now the blackness was complete—the stars only distant pinpoints. "Nothing yet, sir."

The plane had been in the air for over six hours and the boom operator was tired. The mission sounded exciting at first—a mysterious rendezvous and refueling—the tanker carried a classified exotic fuel. But as the hours wore on, he became bored and spent most of the time thinking of overhauling the carburetor on his pickup the next day.

"I see her," he said suddenly. A series of flashing green and red strobes appeared out of the black night converging on the tanker from the west. Although no one had said what kind of aircraft they would be refueling, he had heard the whispers and rumors. Now he knew for sure he was about to get his first look at what only a few had ever seen—the Cirrus.

The successor to the SR-71 Blackbird, the SR-92 Cirrus was the latest product to emerge from the ultra-secret Groom Lake facility at Nellis AFB, Nevada. It was black like the sky that cloaked it—its nose a long needle that extended out of a manta ray-shaped body. The dark visitor dropped into place behind and below the tail-boom operator's position. Then a new voice filled his headset.

"Greetings, Lighthouse. Hope you take credit cards 'cause we're clean out of cash."

"Roger, Slingshot. Your credit's always good with us."

"Then fill her up and check under the hood while you're at it."

The boom operator used a pistol-grip handle to guide the refueling boom out to the open fuel vent on the top of the black plane's fuselage. The nozzle clicked into place and fuel flowed through the hose.

A short time later, the Cirrus's pilot said, "We're topped off, Lighthouse."

"Roger, Slingshot." The boom operator cut the fuel flow. Then he disengaged and retracted the boom.

"Keep the home fires burning, Lighthouse. See you on the flip side."

"Roger, Slingshot. Stay warm." He had heard they were headed for the Arctic.

The black manta ray dropped back, then its nose pitched up. As it passed over the tanker, its green and red strobes were extinguished and the Cirrus became part of the night.

ENTOMBED

The North Atlantic, July

"Looks like a mess of collard greens, don't it?" Billy Manners said as he sat beside Skyler and scrutinized the color radar.

A high-resolution monitor showed the images originating from twenty-two miles overhead. Using low frequency, earth-penetrating technology, the signals from the Cirrus had probed the Greenland ice cap to a depth of six hundred feet surveying thousands of square miles in a matter of minutes. Then, with the threat of sunrise on its heels, the ultra-secret spy plane shot back across the outer fringes of the atmosphere to the protection of its hidden base in the remote Nevada desert.

Skyler smiled at Manners, knowing his friend loved to play the "good ol' country boy" routine. Manners' square poker face was only slightly betrayed by mischievous blue eyes. His simpleminded Georgia-bumpkin façade hid the razor-edged mind of an imaging analyst who left his senior-level post at the CIA's Digital Imagining Division to join

"Skyler's Navy" and "see the world" as he jokingly told everyone.

"Collard greens? That's certainly one way of looking at it, Billy." Skyler chuckled. "But I know there's a slightly more technical version deep inside that analytical mind of yours."

"Yeah, you crazy hillbilly," Mickey Gates said, "don't make us beg." Gates stood behind the two, looking over their shoulders as he sipped a Tecate.

"Well, boys, it's like this," Manners said. "What the glacier gives us is a detailed record of the last hundred thousand years or so of this planet's history—it's sort of like a time machine. You see, over the millennia, each snowfall carries compounds from the air to the ground. The snow piles up in layers and traps the compounds. The tremendous pressure from accumulating snow creates ice that traps bubbles containing minute samples of the atmosphere. Core specimens have pinpointed major events in history like the earliest large-scale pollution started about twenty-five hundred years ago when the Greeks and Romans began mining and smelting lead and silver. And relatively near the surface, there's dust particles from Chernobyl—a tenth of the way down are samples of acid rain caused by volcanic activity when Vesuvius erupted."

"Could we get to the point, Mr. Wizard?" Gates said.

"Keep your britches on, son." Manners took a deep breath before continuing. "Because the ice cap is made up of water, it's relatively easy for radio waves to penetrate. These pictures from your buddies up in that spy bird show us three different kinds of anomalies." He rubbed his four-day growth of beard as he leaned back in the chair. "First, there's the changes in the characteristics of the ice at different depths such as the seventy-foot firn line where granular snow turns into solid glacier ice. We can also see the different layers left by each year's snowfalls. These are a lot like tree rings and are easy to spot because they appear as horizontal lines on the radar's profiles." He pointed at a series of dark green lines spaced fairly evenly across the monitor.

"Second, there are the anomalies within the ice structure itself. These include pockets of solid ice within the granular snow above the firn line and water pockets in the solid glacier ice below the firn line." Manners tapped the screen in a few places to emphasize his geology lesson.

"Finally, there are metal and foreign objects. The profile of a large object like an aircraft below the surface will be elongated like a distinctive rolling hill as opposed to the steep peaks caused by metal fragments and debris closer to the surface."

Like a storyteller around a campfire, he leaned in close to the monitor, slowly extending his finger to a small, dark shape near the bottom. "I'll stake my season tickets to every Georgia Bulldogs home game this year that what you have right there is your missing DC-4, better known as Arctic Air Cargo 101. So, boys, that's the good news."

"And the bad?" Skyler asked.

"She's entombed in solid ice eighty meters down."

RECON

Gates banked the OceanQuest helicopter over the mouth of Scoresby Sund, a fjord that ran some 110 kilometers inland from Greenland's central east coast. At 150 meters above the rocky shore, Skyler sat in the copilot's seat and gazed down at the numerous icebergs still locked in the fast-retreating pack ice. The low angle of the sun reflected a turquoise sheen but their long shadows bore no relation to true size. These were mere babies, he thought, having been in the same region mapping thermal currents a few years before. Then it was early winter and the icebergs were already enormous.

"There's high pressure over all of Greenland," Gates said. "Weather should be perfect for the next few days at least."

Skyler nodded as he looked back at the receding helipad on the aft deck of the *Phoenix*. Their trip up from Woods Hole had been uneventful giving him and his retrieval team plenty of time to plan the excavation and recovery of the korium.

Skyler's first pick for director of the project was his old friend and classmate from the Academy, former naval captain, Jim Hurst. Hurst had worked with OceanQuest on numerous projects including locating the F-117A Stealth Fighter that disappeared on a routine training mission over Montana in 2007. After the Air Force gave up, OceanQuest was called in and located the plane at the bottom of Gold Dust Lake in the remote mountains of Utah. But Hurst was killed in a freak car accident only a day before the *Phoenix* was to sail from Cape Cod.

By coincidence, Rainer Knebel, the managing director of Cape Town Expedition Outfitters of South Africa was visiting Woods Hole and heard about Skyler's search for a project director. After meeting with Skyler and Gates, and presenting his credentials, Knebel was contracted to take Jim Hurst's place.

Rainer Knebel would be responsible for acquiring all the on-site help from the local Inuit population—he had extensive experience on prior expeditions. In addition, all supplies and equipment would be his responsibility.

The rest of the team consisted of experts in arctic geophysics, drilling, and aircraft search and retrieval technology.

As Skyler mulled over details of the operation, he watched a small village pass beneath the helicopter. It resembled a collection of colorful boxes scattered along the shore. He recalled details of the search records given to him by Walter Smyth in London. The last distress call from Arctic Air Cargo mentioned passing over what the pilot thought to be the lights of a small town. Maybe this village was the same one.

At this altitude the air was pristine and Skyler could see miles inland—an expanse of endless white. A thin coastal area separated the frozen wasteland from the sea with shards of greenery and cliffs of ancient rock. Maybe the oldest rocks on the planet, Skyler thought.

It only took twenty minutes before Gates nodded toward the satellite downlink display. "Home sweet home." He banked the helicopter into a low sweeping circle. The flat white glacier swooped up and Gates sat the machine down gently on the ice creating a cloud of swirling powdered snow. The landscape was barren and desolate, broken only by a few low mountain peaks dotting the horizon. The sky was topaz blue.

As the blades of the helicopter slowed and the sound of the turbines wound down, Skyler and Gates opened their side doors, their feet hitting the ice with a crunch.

"Well?" Gates stood with his hands on his hips. He used the toe of his boot to chip away at the crusty frost.

"A deep subject," Skyler said. He slipped on a pair of Serengeti Drivers to protect his eyes from the painful glare. Not a breath of wind stirred in the silence. He paused for a moment absorbing the dramatic vista that lay before him. Then he paced a slow circumference around the helicopter, surveying the area in all directions. It was unusually warm, the temperature hovering in the mid-50s. Skyler's sweater and thermal underwear were almost too much.

Walking all the way around the machine, he stood beside Gates and gazed at a point on the horizon between a pair of distant mountains—a spot Skyler calculated to be about thirty kilometers away.

"Who do you think our friends are?" He watched as a tiny spark of sunlight glinted off the metallic skin of a small airplane passing between the peaks.

"No idea," Gates said, "but they've been shadowing us since we left the coast."

~~~

Dr. Peter Bjoernsson planted his feet firmly on the hard surface of the ice cap as he looked out over the great expanse. Lean and weathered, the fifty-year-old was a glaciologist and arctic expert from the University of Iceland. Behind him lay the OceanQuest base camp—a collection of bright orange dome tents, portable Quonset huts, communications antennae and satellite dishes, snowmobiles, and supply tents. Dark sunglasses protected his eyes from the fierce glare as he glanced down and confirmed the readout on the hand-held GPS. The wind had picked up over the last few minutes and his thinning gray hair swirled haphazardly. "We'll start the grid here," he said to Helen Bermannsson.

The twenty-four-year-old native of Denmark, Bermannsson was Dr. Bjoernsson's understudy. The energetic, petite blond nodded and slipped into the seat of the gleaming red snowmobile. She turned the ignition key producing an instant high-pitched whine as the motor spun to life. A puff of gray smoke shot out its exhaust toward the sled attached to a tether 20 meters to the rear of the vehicle. The sled was about the size of a large Igloo cooler and housed a sub-topographical radar system and a transmitter. It sent radar waves down into the ice as Helen towed it over the surface. When the waves struck an anomaly, they bounced back to the radar's receiver. The former CIA imaging expert, Billy Manners, sitting in the command Quonset hut, could then analyze the signals and create a three-dimensional picture of what lay below.

A second snowmobile sputtered to life—this one driven by a young Icelander named Jon Svensson. Svensson was also a student of Dr. Bjoernsson's. Svensson's radiant white-toothed smile broadcast his excitement at being on his first field expedition. Pulling an identical radar sled, he crisscrossed the grid pattern with Bermannsson, narrowing down the location of the plane.

As the two snowmobiles pulled their sleds into a parallel pattern, Skyler and Rainer Knebel approached Dr. Bjoernsson. "How's it going, Peter?" Skyler asked.

"We did a preliminary run earlier, Sky, just a quick zigzag. She's down there all right." He turned to watch his two assistants' progress. "I'll have an outline of the plane staked out within a couple of hours. As soon as the tractor gets here and we fire up the boiler, we can start dropping the steam probe. By this time tomorrow, I'll have touched your plane with the probe at least a dozen times."

"Excellent," said Skyler. He turned to Knebel. "How long before the tractors arrive?"

"Late tomorrow," the South African said with a slight accent. He was just over six feet with fair skin and thick blond hair. A scar ran across his cheek—a love tap from a leopard, he had told Skyler when the two men first met. During the trip up from Woods Hole and over the two weeks setting up the camp on the ice, Knebel said little, kept to himself and seemed absorbed in the recovery of the ore and the supervision of the Inuits.

They watched the two snowmobiles create a checkerboard pattern across the snow. Then Knebel said, "I've got a dozen Inuit workers coming up with the coring rig and the boiler. They've all had drilling experience on the cap. There's a second tractor with two sixty-five-hundred-watt meltdown diesel generators and enough fuel to run them continuously for a week. Should be more than adequate."

"You'll use Peter's probe holes for guides?" Skyler asked.

Knebel scratched his close-cropped beard. "We'll follow his primary hole with the Vulcan melting a ten-foot-wide shaft straight down. Next, we'll assemble the electric hoist. It's a steel cage large enough to hold five or six men or a nice sized container of ore. It runs up and down on a chain drive inside a metal support frame. Once the hoist is functioning, we'll use steam jet hoses to melt out from the bottom until we've created a cavern exposing the cargo plane."

"You make it sound so easy," Skyler said.

"Only fair to warn you, Sky," Peter Bjoernsson said. "When we get down there, we may find that the millions of tons of ice that have accumulated over so much time have crushed the plane into a sheet of metal no thicker than the Sunday edition of the *New York Times*."

"Let's hope we don't," Skyler said as he felt an icy chill from a blast of Arctic wind.

CARTAGENA MEETING

The armor-plated Mercedes limousine pulled up to the entrance of Demente on an unassuming street corner in the Getsemani neighborhood of Cartagena. Famous for its aged steaks and exotic seafood, Demente was the gathering place of the rich and the ultra-rich like Pablo Escandoza. Each month, he traveled to Cartagena to meet with Alejandro Ramirez, the Director of Banco de National, the largest bank in Colombia, and one of many financial institutions owned by Escandoza. The two men would often dine at Demente.

As Escandoza scrutinized the wine list, Ramirez, a short, balding man in his late fifties said, "I have not seen you smile so much since the day you made the cover of *Fortune* magazine. Have you finally convinced Teresa Castillo that she would be much happier sleeping with you than one of the lesbian fashion models she collects like coins?"

"I should be so lucky," Escandoza said with a sigh. "I'm afraid, Alejandro, that Teresa will spend the rest of her life never wanting or needing what lays between my legs." He flicked his finger and the wine steward who had been waiting a short distance away stepped forward. Escandoza

153

picked an '89 Chateau Latour Blanche and also requested a bottle of Don Perignon to start the evening.

"Very good." The steward bowed before scurrying away.

"Then we truly have something to celebrate?" Ramirez said.

"It is so close, my friend, that I can almost taste it."

"So the last of the hold-outs have put down a deposit?"

"The Blackstone's little demonstration in the sky over Hawaii was more than enough to convince both our customers in South Africa and Iran to commit."

The steward returned and opened the bottle of champagne. After he poured the golden liquid into the crystal flute, he waited for the drug lord's approval.

"Exquisite," Escandoza said with a warm smile.

The steward filled Ramirez's glass and then Escandoza's before leaving the two men alone.

"So what's the latest news from Greenland?" Ramirez asked.

"The salvage company OceanQuest has located the plane and is about to start drilling. The apparatus they will use to recover the korium is being transported to the site with a crew of locals, all handpicked by Rainer Knebel."

"So this man, Knebel, is with the Afrikaner Resistance Movement?"

"An offshoot. One with some very wealthy donors who want things back the way they were. Notice how everyone wants to take their countries back. Anyway, Knebel insisted on protecting his investment in person. He not only arranged for the accidental demise of OceanQuest's project director, but he presented an impressive resume to the director of OceanQuest. It was convincing enough for him to secure the position as new project director. Now the man in charge of the whole recovery operation is our business partner, so to speak."

"He sounds very clever," Ramirez said. "I look forward to meeting him."

"So do I, my friend." Escandoza sipped the champagne. "Once Knebel recovers the korium and eliminates all witnesses from the picture, he will personally escort the ore back to Colombia. I may even consider offering him a permanent position with my organization. We will need resourceful men like him when the delivery process begins."

"I would like to see the faces of the OceanQuest recovery team when they find out Knebel's true identity." Ramirez leaned back in his chair.

"That would be a treat," Escandoza said with a confident smile. "As in all of life, the secret to success is to never let them see you coming."

VULCAN

With a loud hiss and a billowing cloud of steam, the Vulcan probe touched the frozen surface of the glacier. Suspended by steel cables and wenches from a massive derrick, the ten-foot-wide bottom of the cylinder-shaped probe glowed bright red. With the twin diesel meltdown generators roaring as they powered the Vulcan's internal heating elements, the probe began its descent into the ice.

Thick cables and a collection of high-pressure vacuum hoses ran bundled together down into the top of the Vulcan. The cables supplied the electricity for the heating elements that turned the solid ice to boiling water, and the hoses suctioned off the water through a series of intake holes in the probe's head. The water traveled up through the hoses to a pump a few hundred yards away. There it sprayed out over the glacier and turned back into ice.

The Vulcan could melt through thirty feet of ice in a twenty-four-hour period. Working around the clock and with only two minor breakdowns, it took just over nine days before the probe reached the DC-4 260 feet below.

Entombed for over fifty years in the frozen grip of the ice, Arctic Air Cargo 101 once again felt the rush of air on its skin.

"We're there," Dr. Bjoernsson said into the two-way radio.

"Coming, Peter," Skyler answered. He and Gates left the command Quonset hut and walked over to the derrick supporting the Vulcan. They watched as the probe was pulled from the shaft and swung away.

"Would you like to do the honors?" Skyler asked Gates.

"Normally I would say yes, but this is definitely your show, Sky."

With a nod and a broad smile, Skyler strapped on a harness connected to 100 meters of nylon rope. Swinging out over the edge of the shaft, he gave a confident salute before repelling down.

The light on top of his hard hat cast an eerie glow on the translucent walls—the black hole beneath him seemed endless and foreboding. Because the depth of the shaft extended below the water table, the constant dripping made it feel like he was in light rain.

With a thud, Skyler found himself standing on the partially exposed cowling of an airplane engine—its surface was battered and bumpy but intact. The blade of a propeller stuck out of the ice—its paint scarred and the tip bent back, evidence of a hard impact.

"What have you found?" Gates' voice boomed out over the two-way radio strapped to Skyler's waist.

"Contact Chief Inspector Smyth," Skyler said with a grin. "Tell him to pack his bags."

~~~

Based on the motor block's serial number, Skyler confirmed that what he had first stood on was the DC-4's

#2 engine. That meant they had reached the plane's left wing not far from the cockpit. Over the next two days, the hot-water hoses were used to melt through the ice in the direction of the fuselage. Once there, the crew started melting the ice toward the aft of the plane to locate the cargo door.

The glacier had not been kind to Arctic Air Cargo 101, Skyler thought as he stood back watching the slow melting process. The outer skin resembled the surface of the moon, pitted and dented from the force of crushing ice. The #2 engine had moved several inches forward, tearing it from its mounts, linkages and connections. Oil, once contained in the suspended animation of the frozen tomb, now covered the floor of the cave—its alien texture and color seemed to violate the virgin ice. As more of the fuselage was revealed, Skyler realized that even he had underestimated the force of the glacier. The plane had suffered a torturous death.

Over the last week, he had watched Rainer Knebel working with the Inuits. They seemed more than eager to do whatever the South African asked including working in round-the-clock shifts—an unusual characteristic. Skyler had had no such luck with them in the past. The locals usually worked on their own timetable, one that rarely synchronized with the outside world.

It was Rainer Knebel who woke Skyler from a deep sleep at 2:00 a.m. "You asked to be notified when we had the door cleared." Knebel stood in the darkness of Skyler's tent.

"Thanks." He rolled out of his bunk and put on his heavy-weather gear.

It was snowing lightly as he followed Knebel out of the tent and over to the hut protecting the entrance to the shaft. The electric cage hoist was in operation since the shaft was completed, and the two men stepped onto its steel mesh floor. Knebel threw the power switch and the cage shuddered as it started down.

At the bottom, they made their way through the tunnel from the #2 engine to the side of the plane. Moving aft, they entered the cramped chamber where the hot water hoses had uncovered the cargo door. An Inuit used a gas torch to cut the last of the door's outline. Sparks flew everywhere, and Skyler thought they gave the small ice chamber a shimmering ethereal luminescence.

The man switched off the torch and flipped up his protective visor. He turned around smiling to reveal a stubby beard and a mouth full of discolored teeth. A second man stood nearby holding a crowbar. With a nod from Knebel, the man inserted it into the newly cut seam. The resulting metallic screech reminded Skyler of a wounded animal's cry as the large metal door was forced away from the fuselage. The first Inuit picked up another crowbar, working the opposite seam. A few moments later, the door fell with a dull clank onto the oil-stained ice floor. The two Inuits stepped aside as Knebel handed Skyler a lithium ion lantern and moved out of the way.

Skyler took a few steps until he stood at the mouth of the cargo bay. For a second, he was reminded of Howard Carter and how the Egyptian explorer must have felt when he first peered into the just-opened tomb of King Tut. Would he see wondrous things as Carter had or a jumbled mass of wood, wires and sheet metal?

He flicked on the light, and took a cautious step into the fuselage. As his eyes adjusted, he looked at the crumpled ceiling of the plane. It was cracked and bleeding stalactites of ice—the metal girders and supports were bent and twisted. Then he swept the beam revealing not the gold- and jewel-encrusted sarcophagus of an Egyptian pharaoh, but something that certainly would prove even more valuable. Wooden crates—splintered, fractured and somewhat mangled, but miraculously intact—lay before him. The words Niagara Technologies, Buffalo, New York, were stenciled on the sides of each. They contained what Skyler knew would be the lost shipment—five thousand pounds of korium.

He continued swinging the light's beam around the bitter cold cargo bay until it fell on an object in a dark corner near the bulkhead to his right. It was the body of a man sitting on the floor with his back against one of the crates. His limbs were stiff, his skin dark and leathery, an expression of despair on his face. He clutched a faded duffel bag in a frozen embrace.

Skyler aimed the lantern at the corpse. "And you must be Henry Bristol."

ON ICE

A blast of frigid air blew across the icecap like the vengeful sweep of a giant's hand. The blizzard brought with it deep cold and driving snow. For two days, the OceanQuest recovery team hunkered down in their tents waiting for a break in the storm. When the sun finally returned, the removal of the ore was delayed while the entire camp dug itself out.

Before the recovery operation began, Skyler supervised the removal of Henry Bristol's frozen body and had it stored in a packing crate inside a supply tent. The bodies of the pilot and copilot could not be recovered—the nose and cockpit of the DC-4 were crushed. The stolen Barclays half-million pounds were counted and repacked for transfer to Chief Inspector Walter Smyth when he arrived.

For two days, the Inuits brought the korium up a few hundred pounds at a time, placing it in large metal containers on the beds of the two trailers that originally carried the meltdown generators.

As the last of the ore was hoisted to the surface, Skyler stood alone inside the now empty shell of the plane.

161

Earlier, he had discovered a carryall shoved into a small storage compartment—it must have belonged to one of the pilots, he thought. Inside he found a change of clothes, a half-full bottle of English malt whiskey, and an old rusty flare gun. Also some letters from a woman in a town in Scotland and a picture of a young girl, probably the man's daughter. Skyler decided to give the picture and letters to Inspector Smyth. If the girl in the photo was still alive, she might want to know what happened to the owner of the carryall.

Taking a last look around, Skyler headed through the access tunnel to the hoist shaft. The gentle rain from the water table seepage and the muted suction of the siphon pump hoses were the only sounds inside the glacier. Flipping the lever on the control box at the base of the hoist rails, he heard a thump followed by the familiar hum as the mechanism started its descent.

Keying his two-way radio, Skyler said, "Hey, Mick, I think we're ready to shut down this operation and go home." He waited a moment expecting to hear his partner's husky voice bellowing back at him. There was only static. "Mick?" he said. Again, silence. "Just great," He mumbled as he stepped into the cage that had clanked to a halt in front of him. He flipped the lever and the cage started up with a shudder.

It was a three-minute ride to the top. About half way, the water dripping decreased to a trickle and the light from the Greenland mid-day sun grew brighter. He flicked off his lantern and set it at his feet.

Skyler wondered if his radio might be broken as the top of the shaft appeared. When he emerged, he saw Gates and Dr. Bjoernsson standing just to the side of the shaft. They stared back at him with blank expressions, their hands clasped behind their necks. In the same posture of surrender stood Dr. Bjoernsson's two assistants along with imaging expert, Billy Manners. Skyler shifted his gaze to Rainier Knebel and the group of Inuit workers. Each held a machine pistol—Knebel pointed his at Skyler.

"Nice of you to join us," Knebel said.

"What the hell is this?" Skyler took a step forward then stopped.

"A change of plans. You and your crew won't be going back to the coast with us after all. In fact, you'll be staying here with your friend, the bank robber. Now put your hands behind your head." He accented his command with an upward jerk of the gun barrel.

"So you work for Escandoza?" Skyler said.

"No," Knebel said. "Just a concerned customer. I have a lot invested in Escandoza's product and I'm here to protect my investment."

"And you killed Jim Hurst, didn't you?" Mickey Gates said.

"Ever heard the old saying, Mr. Gates, that when something appears too good to be true . . ." Knebel smiled.

"These are innocent people here," Skyler said. "Let them go. You can do whatever you want with me, but killing them serves no purpose."

"Of course it does. It eliminates witnesses." He raised the barrel of the machine pistol. "Now, if you and your friends will be so kind as to get onto the hoist."

"You'll never get away with this," Bjoernsson said as the five men and one woman moved into the cramped cage.

"Enjoy the ride." Knebel flipped the lever causing the hoist to descend. Then he said with a laugh, "Try to stay warm."

He waited until the hoist had traveled the 80 meters and stopped at the bottom. Then he aimed his machine pistol at the junction box housing the hoist's electrical connections, and pulled the trigger. In a quick burst, 9mm slugs ripped the box into a mangled mess. Finally, he walked over to the siphon pumps and turned off the power switch. The motors sputtered and died.

"Now," Knebel said to the Inuits, "we have work to do."

CARAVAN

Chief Inspector Walter Smyth looked down from the window of the de Havilland Beaver and wondered whatever possessed him to get in the ancient little plane in the first place. He hated flying even in jumbo jets—this was his worst fear. His pilot could not be over sixteen. Acne covered his face and he chewed bubble gum nonstop, blowing and popping it to the total irritation of the inspector.

This had been the only plane for hire at the tiny airstrip outside the town of Kuummiut, because it was the height of tourist season. All the other planes were being used for sightseeing and fishing expeditions. After stowing his passenger's bag, the boy had motioned for Smyth to get in and buckle up. On the third try, the tired old engine coughed to life and the boy taxied to the end of the dirt runway. Smyth, who was not a church-going man, was praying aloud as the final one hundred meters of the airstrip approached. At the last possible second, the plane lumbered into the pristine blue sky, heading west toward the great expanse of Greenland's interior.

"So your friends are looking for the old cargo plane?" the boy said. They had left the coast and were cruising along at five thousand feet.

"Yes." Smyth tried to warm his hands in the trickle of hot air coming through the rusted heater vent.

"Legend has is that it's buried under a million tons of ice."

"I wouldn't know." Smyth watched the endless snow and ice fields pass beneath.

"What do they want with that old piece of junk, anyway?"

"I suppose they want it for a museum or something." Smyth's teeth chattered. He was more uncomfortable than he could ever remember.

"Seems like a waste of time to me."

A few black dots on the white horizon caught the inspector's eye and he pointed. "What's that?"

The boy pulled a pair of binoculars from under his seat. "Looks like tractors."

Smyth took the binoculars and adjusted them to his vision. He saw two huge Caterpillar tractors pulling long trailers—their cargo piled high and covered with tarpaulins. Two smaller snow cats followed behind, their metal treads throwing up white powder. Smyth counted half a dozen men riding on the bed of each. Within a couple of minutes, the caravan passed underneath the Beaver. Smyth noticed that none of the men bothered to wave as the small plane flew overhead.

"Friendly bunch." Smyth rubbed his hands together for warmth and squinted as he searched for any sign of the OceanQuest camp. His pulse quickened at the thought that he might soon come face to face with Henry Bristol, the man who murdered his father. The message from Matt Skyler had said only that they located the plane. There was no confirmation of finding the corpse. Skyler predicted that they would reach the plane by the time the Chief Inspector had arrived from London. Smyth trembled at what might lay ahead.

"There it is," the boy-pilot said and pointed.

Smyth looked out the side window as the plane banked to the right and the OceanQuest base camp came into view. Against the stark white glare of the snow, he saw the bright orange dome tents and Quonset huts, the communications antennae and satellite dishes, and the huge generators that powered the Vulcan probe Skyler had told him about. Why was no one coming out to greet them? Couldn't Skyler and his crew hear the roar of the Beaver as it circled the camp? Where were the scientists and drilling crews?

As the small plane dropped closer to the frozen surface of the glacier, a chill as cold as the arctic itself ran up Smyth's spine. Something was wrong, he thought, staring down at the lifeless camp. Something was definitely wrong.

FLARE

"I don't want to sound pessimistic," Gates said as the echoes of the automatic weapons fire died at the bottom of the shaft, "but we're in deep shit."

"Deep water would be more like it." Skyler swung his lantern in the direction of the tunnel.

"We've got to find a heat source," Gates said.

Skyler thought for a moment. "The torch!"

"Exactly," Gates said.

Skyler led the group down the tunnel toward the entrance to the plane's cargo bay. The gas tanks and welding torch used to open the cargo door were still pushed into a corner out of the way. He held the light as Gates opened the valve and snapped the flint that ignited the flame.

"It's not much, folks, but it's all we got." Gates turned the valve wide open, and the heat from the flame radiated out as the group circled around it.

Skyler's mind raced, calculating all possible escape routes. The hoist was useless—he'd already tried the power switch and assumed the gunfire was Knebel blowing the control box to shreds. First priorities were to keep warm and dry, two things that were now next to impossible. The constant seepage of water was unstoppable. Without the pumps, it would turn to slush and then back to ice—layer after layer until the entire tunnel and plane filled and froze. He knew if he didn't do something fast, they were all destined to die of hypothermia long before they would be entombed in the glacier ice.

"I going to climb out," he announced after considering all the other options.

"The rails only serve as guides for the hoist," Peter Bjoernsson said, his words rattling like marbles in his mouth from the extreme cold. "They're only lightweight tubing and won't stand up to your weight."

"Unless you've got a better idea, Peter," Skyler said, "the only way out is up that shaft. We have no choice."

"You'll need something to use as a harness," Gates said.

"We can use some of the scraps from the wreckage." Skyler flipped the lantern on. While the rest of the group stayed huddled around the torch, the two men moved along the length of the plane's interior picking up pieces of broken wood and metal. There were shards of glass, lengths of jagged conduit, huge knots of cables, wires, and hydraulics. They had to stoop in the area where the roof partially caved in.

Skyler kicked a splintered piece of crating out of his way, and then picked up a large mass of cable. "Looks like enough here to bind together and secure me to the hoist rail."

Gates thought for a moment then bent over to examine the heavy-gage wire. "It just might work." He yanked on it testing its strength.

The two men pulled and tugged at the mass of wire until they had separated enough pieces to assemble a makeshift harness. They took all the pieces back through the passage to the base of the shaft. Working quickly, they fashioned two harnesses—one to secure Skyler to the railing and a second to pull himself up the framework a foot or two at a time.

The tube frame secured the rails and chain drive—each horizontal tube was spaced about three feet apart. When he was ready, Skyler tied the end of the first wire harness to the frame over his head and stepped up on the thin tubing. Holding the rails, he bounced slightly and waited for the worst. But the tube held. He pulled himself up to the next tube easing his full weight down. There was a slight creaking sound and the aluminum bent in the middle, but held.

"So far so good," he said and smiled down at Gates eight meters below.

Moving the second harness up and securing it, he unfastened the first and pulled himself to the next rung. Feeling confident, he let his weight down on the tube and was about to untie the lower harness when the fragile aluminum bent and snapped. Skyler tumbled down through the frame hitting with a thud on the ice floor. His heavy weather outfit protected him from serious injury but the wind was knocked out of his lungs as he lay in five inches of ice water.

Gates reached under Skyler's arms and helped him to his feet. "Guess it's time to go to plan B."

"Which is?" Skyler stood.

"I have no idea."

"Then we'll have to try it again." Skyler examined the remnants of his harness.

He had just removed the wires from around his waist when he hesitated and cocked his head. "Did you hear that?"

"I sure did." Gates stared up the shaft.

Skyler ran back through the tunnel, his boots splashing in the freezing slush. With the beam of the lantern swinging haphazardly, he shot past the small group huddled around the torch and went straight to the small storage locker containing the pilot's carryall he had found earlier. Sifting through it, he grabbed the flare gun and cartridge, and headed back.

"What's wrong, Sky?" Billy Manners asked, his eyes wide.

"Have you found a way out?" Helen Bermannsson asked in a meek, high-pitched voice.

"Say a prayer this thing fires," Skyler shouted over his shoulder as he held the flare gun up. Coming to a splashing halt beside his partner, he positioned himself in the middle of the shaft and planted his feet shoulder wide. He loaded the cartridge and gripped the flare gun with both hands, then raised his arms over his head. Aiming the barrel at a distant dot of blue sky barely visible through the mist of water seepage, he pulled back the hammer and squeezed the trigger.

Click.

"Damn!" He held the gun at arm's length. "Shine the lantern on it."

Gates aimed the beam on the gun as Skyler broke the barrel open and examined the cartridge. There was a thin coating of rust covering where the firing pin would strike. He pulled the cartridge out, wiping it on his coat—a brown smear marked the spot. Then he rammed the flare back in the chamber, slammed the gun shut, cocked the hammer, and again took aim.

Click.

"Let me see it." Gates broke open the gun and pulled back the hammer. He quickly discovered a coating of rust covered it as well. Taking a small knife from his pocket, he cleaned the end of the pin. Leaving the hammer in the firing position, he closed the gun and handed it back.

Once again, Skyler aimed it over his head and squeezed the trigger.

BLAM!

With a deafening, throaty whoosh, the flare burst from the barrel like a Roman Candle. The flame lit the opaque ice walls with a surreal glow. For a moment, Skyler thought he had just released the ghost of Arctic Air Cargo 101.

A few seconds later, he heard the distant muffled boom as the flare ignited in the air over the mouth of the shaft. Then just as quickly, the shaft fell back into the monotonous patter of the dripping water.

"What's going on?" Peter Bjoernsson called as he led the others down the tunnel to join Skyler and Gates.

"We thought we heard the sound of a prop plane," Skyler said.

"You mean there's someone up there?" Helen asked.

"Someone besides that son-of-a bitch, Knebel," Billy Manners added.

"You guys get back to the torch," Skyler said. "We're going to try climbing out again."

Peter Bjoernsson motioned for the group to return to the cargo bay.

Suddenly, the two-way radio attached to Skyler's belt crackled and hissed to life. A strange voice, distant and thin, said, "Hello? Anyone there?"

Skyler yanked the radio off his belt with such force that he broke the clasp. "Yes," he yelled into the device. "We're here! Who are you?"

172

There was a long pause as the group took in a collective breath and held it.

"I'm Chief Inspector Walter Smyth." The words were half-buried in the static white noise from transmitting through the thick ceiling of ice. "Who's there?"

Surrounded by an immediate outburst of whoops and hollers, Skyler held the radio to his mouth, shouting, "It's my turn to buy, Walter."

BACK ON THE SURFACE

"That's the sweetest sound I've ever heard," Gates said as the hiss of the suction pumps filled the tunnel at the bottom of the shaft. "Remind me to give that guy a big kiss."

"I was thinking of calling the Vatican and nominating him for sainthood," Skyler said. He secured his foot firmly in the loop at the end of the rope dropped down by Smyth. Then he radioed the inspector to pull him up. Five minutes later Skyler emerged from the shaft shoving a grateful hand at Smyth. "You're truly a sight for sore eyes, Walter."

"My wife always said I had perfect timing." The pudgy little Englishman gave a sly smile. To pull Skyler up, he had secured the rope to a snowmobile and let the boy-pilot do the driving.

"She'll get no argument from me," Skyler said.

As the boy circled the snowmobile back to where the two men stood, Skyler inspected what was left of the electrical switch box controlling the power to the hoist.

"What do you think?" Smyth asked.

"Knebel shot it up pretty bad but I can repair it. I guess he didn't anticipate you coming along to rescue us or he would have destroyed everything."

174

Skyler retrieved a tool kit from the command hut and within ten minutes had mended and spliced the wires back together. While Smyth and the boy watched, Skyler reattached the generator cables and flipped the power switch. The hoist motor hummed. Then he radioed down for the rest of his crew to climb on. Soon, Gates and the others emerged from the shaft.

"They've got quite a head start," Gates said once the group had gathered in the warmth of the command hut.

"There may still be time to catch up and find out how they plan to get the korium back to Colombia," Skyler said.

"Think they'll use some kind of air transport?" Dr. Bjoernsson asked.

"Maybe, but my guess is a freighter—small nondescript, and innocent looking."

"We passed over a group of tractors pulling heavy cargo on trailers on our way here," Smyth said.

"That was them," Gates said.

"Knebel did us a favor by wrecking the satellite communications before he left," Billy Manners said. "The *Phoenix* will realize by now that there's no data link."

"They *will* send the helicopter?" Dr. Bjoernsson asked.

"Eventually," Skyler said. "But we can't wait." He studied a detailed map of the coastline spread out on a table. "Once that ore is loaded on a freighter, they could drop out of the shipping lanes and disappear." He turned to the boy. "Do you have a radio on your plane?"

"Busted." The boy popped his bubble gum.

Skyler turned back to the map. "All right, here's what we'll do. Mick and I'll fly back to the coast with our young friend here. Once we determine how Knebel is transporting the korium, we'll head for Scoresby Sund and get word to the *Phoenix* to notify Argentine and put the military on alert."

175

"The generators work and there's plenty of fuel and provisions," Gates said to the rest of the group. "Just stay warm and hold on. We'll get help back here as soon as possible."

Skyler turned to Smyth. "Inspector, we can't thank you enough."

"It works both ways," Smyth said. "Now I know beyond a doubt what happened to my father and the stolen money. That's thanks enough to last a lifetime." After final farewells, Skyler, Gates, and the boy climbed into the Beaver. With a great deal of sputtering and coughing, the old plane taxied to a flat area of the snowfield, lumbered across the ice and lifted into the blue sky. The OceanQuest crew waved as the Beaver made a final circle over their heads before setting a course due east.

Dr. Peter Bjoernsson walked over to the shaft entrance and flipped off the power to the pumps. "Rest in peace, Arctic Air Cargo 101." After the drone of the Beaver faded, the only sound was the crunch of boots on the snow as he and the others headed back to the warmth of the command hut.

COLD BAY

Along a barren stretch of Greenland's eastern coast, twenty kilometers from the nearest settlement stood what remained of Cold Bay Fishery. It was a collection of rundown, weathered buildings long abandoned and forgotten. The once thriving factory lay exposed to the harsh Arctic weather like an aged boxer on the mat for the last time. A nearby town, home to the cannery workers decades earlier, was deserted. A few remnants of canvas flapping in the wind and bits of timber sticking up from the wild summer grass were all that remained. The main cannery building sat on a rocky ledge overlooking a long wooden dock jutting into the ocean like a feeble finger. Other than an Arctic hare or a small rodent, Cold Bay was lifeless.

The two Caterpillar tractors pulling the trailers heavy with containers of korium rumbled up to the old main building. Knebel jumped from the cab of the lead tractor and shouted to his crew, "We must move fast. Get the cargo off the trailers and into the building as quickly as possible. We have to be ready to make the transfer."

The Inuit workers unhitched the tie-down straps from the flatbeds of the trailers and rolled the containers down metal ramps. Placing each on a dolly, they pushed the precious cargo into the cavernous shell of the factory. Within an hour, all the containers were piled near the rear doors where the fresh North Atlantic cod had once been brought in for processing. The tractors were then stored out of sight in a warehouse a few hundred meters from the factory. As the soft glow of the sun neared the horizon throwing the Arctic into summer night twilight, Knebel and his workers waited.

~~~

Skyler could see the deep blue of the North Atlantic stretching across the horizon as they approached the coast. The snow-covered ice cap fell away, replaced by a fragile strip of brown and gray vegetation that managed somehow to survive a few months of the year in the harsh environment.

"Let's climb to five thousand and head south," Skyler said.

"Why south?" the boy asked as he brought the nose up banking to the right.

"Too many villages to the north," Gates said, sitting behind the pilot. "Our friends would attract attention." He searched the sparse landscape with his binoculars. A single dirt road wound along the coast beneath them.

"I'm gonna have to refuel soon," the boy said.

"How much time left?" Skyler asked.

"Twenty minutes tops." He gave Skyler a shrug as he tapped the fuel gauge.

"Hold everything, I got them." Gates pointed to a spot along the dirt road four or five kilometers ahead as a flash of light reflected off one of the tractors. "Looks like they're headed for some buildings right on the coast."

"What is that place?" Skyler asked the boy.

"Cold Bay. Used to be a fishery. Nothing but a ghost town now."

"And a perfect place to load their cargo on a ship," Gates said.

"Take us back over the cap before they spot us," Skyler said.

The boy banked to the right heading inland.

"See those hills?" Skyler pointed.

Rising out of his seat, the boy looked and nodded.

"Let's find a place to put her down on the other side. Looks like no more than a couple of kilometers—an easy hike back to Cold Bay." He glanced over his shoulder at Gates.

"Walk in the park," Gates said and nodded.

Ten minutes later, the Beaver touched down on a flat snowfield, blowing up clouds of white as the engine revved and the plane stopped. Skyler pulled two one-hundred-dollar bills from his wallet and handed them to the boy. "Go refuel and be back here as soon as you can."

"No problem." He grinned and shoved the money in his jacket pocket.

Shielding their eyes from the snow-filled backwash, Skyler and Gates waited as the Beaver swung around and lifted back up into the late afternoon sky. It banked north and disappeared beyond the distant hills.

"Shall we?" Mickey Gates said with a sweep of his arm.

"After you," Skyler said as they set out at a steady pace across the ice.

~~~

Moisture from the south settled in over the coast in the form of a thick fog bank as Skyler and Gates entered the ghost town. The fog gave the landscape a deep gray blanket, masking the dim twilight of the Arctic summer into almost total darkness. Moving cautiously between the empty shells of the small wooden-frame houses, they crept across the sparse grass and spongy mosses until they lay flat on the ground beside a storage building fifty meters from the cannery.

After waiting thirty minutes with no sign of movement, Gates said, "You want to take a closer look?"

"I always prefer front row seats." With only starlight to guide them, they slipped across the field and stood with their backs against the outside of the factory. "I'm going to work my way around front and see if I can get inside. You check out the back."

With a nod, Gates disappeared into the thick fog as Skyler moved along the outside wall looking for an opening. He didn't have to search long. A window, its panes gone, the wooden frame rotten and brittle, opened like a dark wound. Skyler boosted himself over the sill and quietly dropped down onto a hard floor. The blackness seemed empty and eternal, but he knew somewhere inside was Knebel, the Inuits, and the korium.

~~~

Gates felt his way along the side of the building, careful not to trip over the scattered debris under the thick weeds. He was about to step over a pile of timber when instinct made him hesitate.

Crouched beside what may have once been a loading dock, he turned and stared in the direction of the old fishery wharf. Like a weak signal from a distant TV station, the faint outline of a long dark shape appeared through the fog. Suddenly, a blinding spotlight split the grayness, its beam sweeping up the dock and across the rear of the cannery building. Gates dropped flat on the ground, his eyes seeing but his mind not wanting to acknowledge what appeared before him.

For an instant, the fog thinned. At the end of the dock where cod-laden fishing boats once unloaded their catch sat the menacing form of a Yankee-class Soviet nuclear submarine. A black pirate flag snapped in the wind.

"I don't believe it," he whispered. "They've got two boomers."

Then he heard the gunfire.

THE DEATH OF MATT SKYLER

There were voices, panic-filled and desperate. Skyler could not hear them clearly, but he knew they were pleas for mercy. Feeling his way along a wall and around a corner, he saw a large room—the orange glow of a lantern lit a small area in the middle. He spotted the many containers of ore, each about the size of a 55-gallon oil drum, sitting on the far fringe of the dim pool of light—ready for their journey to South America. The Inuit workers were huddled together facing Skyler's direction, their hands in the air. In between, with his back to Skyler, was Knebel. He held a machine pistol aimed at the Inuits—a pile of weapons at his feet.

Knebel raised his gun and took aim causing the Inuits' cries to increase in volume and urgency. In the next instant, flame shot from the barrel as he emptied the clip.

Skyler watched the workers drop. Most appeared to be killed immediately, some squirming and twitching in their last death throes.

As quickly as the slaughter began, it was over. A heavy silence filled the empty space once the echoes of the machine pistol faded. Knebel pulled the clip from the gun and replaced it with a fresh one. Enveloped by a pale cloud of gunpowder smoke, he stood over the bodies, searching for any signs of life. With short bursts, he finished any victim still struggling to survive.

Suddenly, a flood of light swept across the outside of the building, streaming white light through cracks and broken windows. Knebel turned his attention to it and moved to stand beside the ore containers. He stared out a window toward the ocean.

With the South African distracted, Skyler came out of his concealment and covered the space between him and the pile of weapons. He grabbed a shotgun and then backed away into the darkness. Knebel returned to the middle of the room—a carryall bag lay beside the guns. He bent to pick it up, but froze.

"The inside of a glacier is a very cold place." Skyler stepped from the shadows.

A momentary look of surprise flashed across Knebel's face. But it faded back to an expression of disregard. "You're more resourceful that I imagined." He straightened—the gun at his side in one hand and the carryall in the other.

"And you are a ruthless murderer." Skyler aimed the shotgun.

"This was strictly business—nothing personal." Knebel smiled crookedly.

"Tell that to the families of those men." Skyler nodded at the mangled heap of dead bodies.

"I'm a professional. I have a job to do and I do it." Knebel glanced over his shoulder for an instant toward the containers, then back to Skyler. "I suggest you drop your weapon and surrender. You'll never leave here alive if you don't."

"There is one other option."

With a thud, the carryall hit the floor. As the South African pulled the barrel of the machine pistol into a firing position, Skyler's shotgun boomed. The blast slammed into Knebel's face, ripping it into torn flesh and splintered bone.

Knebel squeezed the trigger of the machine pistol sending a white-hot stream of bullets arcing into the air. The second blast of Skyler's shotgun crushed Knebel's head and his body dropped into a heap on the ground. With a final twitch, his muscles convulsed, then stilled.

Skyler stood over the body pointing the 12-gauge at the dead man—a trail of smoke snaked from the barrel. Knebel's own mother wouldn't recognize him, Skyler thought, looking at what was once a face. He was about to slip back into the shadows to find Gates when a voice called out.

"Don't move!" It was deep and authoritative, and filled the hollow emptiness of the old cannery.

Skyler stiffened and tightened his grip on the shotgun.

"Drop your gun," the voice commanded.

It slipped from Skyler's hands and hit hard on the dirt floor.

"Put your arms up and turn around slowly."

He did as he was told. In the dim light of the lantern, he saw five men dressed in naval-style uniforms, each aiming a weapon.

The leader stepped forward until he was only a few feet away. He glanced at the body on the floor—steaming blood still oozing from the wounds. Looking at Skyler again, he walked over to the bullet-riddled bodies of the Inuits. After a moment, he returned, this time his gun lowered. "So, Mr. Knebel. I got your message that you would be eliminating the Inuits as soon as we arrived, but who is this one?" He gestured to the body.

Hesitating only a second, Skyler said, "That's what's left of the Director of OceanQuest, Matt Skyler."

TIGER SHARK

"Escandoza has a second sub, sir." White House Chief of Staff Nathan Templeton stood in front of the President's desk. "It's disappeared in the North Atlantic with the korium on board."

The President stared back in silence, his hand stopped writing his notes. "My God. This is confirmed?"

"Yes, sir." Templeton tensed.

"Satellite surveillance tracked the sub leaving the coast of Greenland before it submerged," said Thomas Lancaster. The Secretary of the Navy had accompanied Templeton into the Oval Office. "Our SOSUS listening stations along the continental shelf are trying to establish contact."

"How in the hell did he get a second . . .?" The President wiped his hand across his chin, already knowing the answer—just another business expense for the richest man in the world. "We should have said screw you to Denmark and gone into Greenland with a company of Seals to protect OceanQuest."

"And caused a major international incident," Templeton said.

The President stared at him. "I can assure you, Thomas, if that sub makes it to Colombia, I'm not going to ask anyone's permission to go in and crush Escandoza."

"We hope it won't come to that, sir," Lancaster said.

The President sighed. "Why didn't you know about it? Destroy it before it even got to Greenland?"

"We had no clue that Escandoza had a second boat. Nothing in our intelligence led us to consider that possibility. We just weren't looking in the right direction."

"Then *start* looking in the right direction, Thomas. Either capture or sink it."

"It's not quite that cut and dry, Mr. President." Lancaster eased down into one of the two chairs in front of the President's desk. "We're talking hundreds, perhaps thousands of commercial surface vessels between Greenland and Colombia, and possibly dozens of submarines. Some are from the former Soviet Navy, the same type as the pirate sub. Confronting the wrong one would lead to a serious problem or embarrassment. To be honest, sir, finding and destroying any modern warship is difficult. But our strategic sensors are focused on that task. We've formed a 100 kilometer circle around the last known position and started dropping sonobuoys along the expected route. We've laid out a search pattern that will provide the highest potential for pinpointing the sub's location. Our land-based ASW aircraft are ready to concentrate on any contact before the sub has a chance to escape."

"I don't like that word—escape." The President felt his patience wearing thin.

"It's a relative term, sir," Lancaster said.

Slamming his hand down on the desk, the President said, "Hunt the damn thing down and destroy it. Is that understood?"

Templeton gave Lancaster a quick glance before saying, "There's something we haven't told you, sir."

The President glared at the Chief of Staff.

"Matt Skyler is on board."

~ ~ ~

The *Carupano* plowed through the heavy swells of the North Atlantic, black smoke pouring from its funnel. Registered to a Panamanian shipping firm, the 142-foot freighter carried diesel tractors and road graders manufactured in the United Kingdom along with irrigation pumps from Portugal. Its captain, a bull of a man named Sampson, watched from the bridge as the dark storm swept in, churning the ocean. Rain pelted the windows and the wind howled like a wounded animal. Sampson steadied himself as the deck rolled. He looked at his first officer beside him. "We're in for a rough ride."

"We've seen worse, captain," the smaller man said with little enthusiasm as he tried to sip his jiggling cup of coffee.

Sampson shrugged and walked away. "I'll be in my cabin if you need me."

Ten minutes later, the captain lay on his bunk watching "Confessions of a Call Girl" on his iPad. He had watched it a dozen times since leaving port and no longer felt an arousal at the sight of the women spreading themselves before him. As he turned the tablet off and stared at the ceiling, he wondered why he had been ordered to leave Liverpool so quickly with two major cargo shipments still sitting in the warehouse. And why the ridiculous route across the North Atlantic, an area of the ocean he detested? He must travel thousands of miles out of the way costing him wasted days. It made no sense at all. But there was one consolation: triple pay. The first time the company had ever offered it. For that kind of money, the captain admitted before drifting off to sleep, he would sail to Colombia by way of Sydney.

~~~

The knot in the pit of Skyler's stomach tightened as he stood in the control room of the missile submarine watching the activity around him. Surrounded by the enemy reminded him of the huge capture-the-flag games he played at the academy. The game covered acres of Maryland backwoods—one team's flag on a small island surrounded by a frigid creek, and the other in a deep, rocky gorge half a kilometer away. In the championship game of his senior year, Skyler had switched jerseys with a captured soldier and sneaked into the opposition's camp, stole the flag and won the trophy for his classmates. He felt that same knot in his stomach as he stood on the bridge of the pirate sub.

Dominating the middle of the control room was the periscope pedestal containing the Officer of the Deck watch station and two periscopes. To Skyler's left were five men seated at the fire control consoles. To the right, the helmsman, planesman, and diving officer manned the control stations and navigational systems. An automated plotting table was on the opposite side of the periscope pedestal. The room hummed with electronics.

"Welcome to the *Tiger Shark*, Mr. Knebel," said the man standing beside the OOD watch station. He was well over six feet and skeleton thin, his eyes dark holes recessed into his head. His blond hair, in need of a trim, was combed straight back. He walked to Skyler, extending a bony hand. "I'm Captain Helmet Schafer. You look familiar, have we met?"

"Perhaps," Skyler said, shaking the German's hand. He cringed at the thought of how his picture had appeared often in the world press. "I've represented my organization on a few local Johannesburg television talk shows."

"Yes, I'm sure that's it. Have you settled into your cabin?"

"A bit small, but it will do." He tried to project Knebel's arrogance.

"Something you have to get used to down here." Schafer made a broad sweep of his hand. "Every square inch is needed for our electronic systems. There's very little room left for comfort."

As a former Navy Lieutenant Commander, Skyler was more than aware of shipboard confinement although he had never spent time on missile subs, only raised them from the ocean floor after they sank.

"I understand things went well at Cold Bay." Schafer said.

"If you mean there are no witnesses left."

"Something like that." Schafer chuckled. "Neat and tidy, that's what I demand."

"So how long until our final destination?"

"Normally a little over eight days. But we are going to have to go a bit slower on this trip."

"Problem?"

"Nothing you need to be concerned with, Mr. Knebel." Schafer smiled and sat down in the captain's chair. "Purely a military maneuver. Why don't you rest in your cabin until dinner? Then you can join me. I'm anxious to learn all about your organization—the Afrikaner Resistance Movement, is it called?"

"Yes." Skyler turned to leave the bridge. He had been briefed a few months previous on racist organizations, and the South African group had been one of them. He'd also visited their Web site and seen their hate literature. He tried to remember details. His father had always told him he should have been an actor.

Now he was getting his chance.

RUN SILENT

"Ah, there you are." Captain Schafer looked up smiling. "Please sit down, Mr. Knebel."

Skyler stepped into the small, private dining room and took a place opposite Schafer. The two men were alone.

"Help yourself." Schafer pointed to a bottle of Schloss Castel Muller Kabinett. "This is from the Mosel region. It's slightly drier than wine from the Rhine. I hope you like it."

Skyler poured the pale German wine into his glass and took a sip. "Refreshing."

"I prefer their Auslese, but it would be a little too heavy with dinner.

"Are you from the Mosel region?"

"Actually Wiesbaden, near Frankfurt." Schafer said. "My father was a diesel mechanic, my mother a nurse. And you?"

"Born in Munich, but we moved to Pretoria when I was a small boy. My father was a school teacher, my mother stayed home trying to keep us in line."

"Both honorable positions in life, my friend." Schafer smiled and gestured with his glass. "And today we sit across from one another pondering the world."

"To pondering." Skyler returned the toast.

The door opened and a young seaman entered carrying a tray. He placed a bowl of soup in front of each man and left.

"A hearty meal of potato soup." Schafer motioned with his spoon for Skyler to start.

Skyler resisted wiping his forehead and hoped the captain would not notice his uneasiness. Maybe the conversation would stay casual and not delve into the Afrikaner Resistance Movement.

"Tell me about your group," Schafer said between spoonfuls.

Skyler tasted the soup, buying time to collect his thoughts. "We have about five thousand members mostly in South Africa, but some in other parts of the world. We're fortunate to have some wealthy contributors who are generous with their support, allowing us to carry out our work."

"Which is?"

"In its simplest form, the preservation of the white race by any means, individually and collectively, as a people of God."

"A holy war, then?"

Skyler sipped the wine. "We fight to safeguard the existence of our race, the sustenance of our children, the purity of our blood, and the freedom and independence of our people. We do it to fulfill the mission allotted to us by the Creator of the universe." Skyler took another spoonful of soup. "This is delicious."

"My mother used to make potato soup along with thick, crusty salt bread. I still don't know why we all weren't as big as elephants growing up on meals like this." Schafer paused, giving Skyler a stern look. "So what do you plan to do with your Candle?"

"Cleansing." Skyler smiled over the bowl at the captain. "Mass cleansing, of course."

"And once you have . . . cleansed?"

"Then we take back our country." He was about to go into his rehearsed speech on why whites are the superior race when the intercom on the wall squawked.

"Captain to the bridge!" the metallic voice called.

Schafer rose and pushed the talk-back button. "What is it? I'm eating."

"We have contact, sir."

"Our friend?"

"Yes."

"All right, I'm coming." The captain turned to Skyler. "Mr. Knebel, you must excuse me. We are about to rendezvous with another vessel and I am needed on the bridge. Continue enjoying your dinner."

"I'd like to tag along if you don't mind. I'm intrigued with your impressive ship and its complex inner workings."

Schafer paused for a moment. "I'll instruct my steward to keep our meals warm for us." He opened the door for Skyler. "You might even find this entertaining."

~~~

The private Gulfstream banked into the setting sun as it made its final approach to the small airport on the northern tip of San Andres Island, the main island in the Caribbean archipelago. It was remote—700 kilometers northwest of the Colombian mainland and 230 east of Nicaragua.

Pablo Escandoza gazed down on the slender, finger-shaped strip of land glistening like an emerald in the sunset. Coconut palms almost entirely covered its hilly terrain. The lights of the town of San Andres sparkled in the twilight as they passed beneath.

The town's heritage dated back to 1527 when Spanish explorers settled there. Serving as a pirate stronghold for decades, the legendary Henry Morgan recognized its strategic location and established his base while waiting to sack gold-laden galleons bound for home. Escandoza often thought of himself as a pirate of the highest order.

"We're getting closer to our final destination, William," Escandoza said. "From San Andres, we travel by boat to a smaller island about an hour from here. I think you'll find your new home nothing short of paradise."

William Thorpe, his tired face showing the rigors of too little sleep and a constant dependency on prescription drugs, sat across from Escandoza. He turned and stared out the window.

The drug lord studied the 70-year-old scientist. Even in the chilly, dry air of the jet, the man's shirt revealed sweat stains. Thorpe's health had declined over the last month— he had lost a considerable amount of weight. Escandoza decided he would assign a physician to keep Thorpe alive long enough to complete the manufacture of the Candles. Once the process was documented and taught to the drug lord's handpicked team of technicians, there would be no further need for the former member of Project Candle Power. Perhaps he would bury Dr. Thorpe right here on San Andres, Escandoza thought. He might even build a monument to the sad, little man responsible for changing the world forever.

Teresa Castillo sat on the circular couch in the back of the small jet. Her dark hair, shinning like polished ebony, fell around her shoulders as she crossed her tanned legs. She looked up from the *London Financial Times,* and smiled. "You'll like the island, Dr. Thorpe. It's beautiful."

Her companion, a sixteen-year-old stripper from Rio de Janeiro named Krystal, stirred beside her. The girl had slept the entire flight from Colombia and now sat up stretching.

She was angelic, Escandoza thought, as he admired the teen's tiny bare feet with nails screaming cherry red. "Teresa is right, it's very beautiful." He reluctantly turned his attention back to Thorpe. "The lab is almost complete, and the korium is scheduled for delivery a week from today. You have only to supervise the final preparations so we can begin production as soon as the *Tiger Shark* arrives."

"Fine," Thorpe said dryly. He returned to making notes in a binder he carried.

There was a slight bump as the Gulfstream touched down and rolled the length of the runway. It slowed and turned toward two cars parked along the tarmac. One was a black Mercedes limousine, the other a dark gray, windowless van. The jet taxied to a stop and the side door opened and swung down to form steps. Colonel Blackstone emerged from the van and approached the jet. He reached up and offered his hand to Teresa who ignored him as she stepped down onto the asphalt. Krystal accepted the colonel's offer and smiled at the rugged-looking mercenary as she gingerly placed her spiked sandals on each step. Once the two women were together, they walked hand-in-hand to the big German-built car.

William Thorpe followed giving Blackstone only a momentary glance.

At last, Escandoza filled the entrance to the plane at the top of the steps. "Good evening, Colonel."

"Teresa's latest piece of candy?"

"Yes." The two men shook hands once Escandoza stood on the tarmac. "I can only assume she is as delicious as she looks." He turned and saluted his pilot. Then he started toward the limousine with Blackstone at his side. "What is the latest?"

"I have good news and a little surprise."

Escandoza smiled, his white linen suit blowing in the brisk tropical breeze. "Don't keep me in suspense." He brushed the hair from his eyes.

"The *Tiger Shark* is underway, the korium safe and secure. That's the good news."

"And the surprise?"

"We have a special guest on board."

"Not Rainer Knebel?"

"No. Unfortunately, Mr. Knebel was killed in a shootout at the last moment."

"Then who?"

"Someone we both have wanted to meet for a long time."

Escandoza stopped and stared at Blackstone. "Skyler?"

"He shot Knebel and is masquerading as the South African."

"Really?" Escandoza chuckled.

"Captain Schafer recognized him right away but is taking no action unless we request it."

"So Mr. Skyler has become a real annoyance."

"Should I order the captain to eliminate him? Having Skyler alive is one more problem we don't need."

"We have no problems, Colonel, only opportunities. I've always believed that if you want to punish someone, really make them suffer, you need to know what they value." A broad smile swept across the drug lord's face. "And then you take it away."

~~~

"Give me an electronic sweep." Captain Schafer eased into his chair in the command center of the *Tiger Shark*.

Skyler stood behind him watching the sophisticated order in which the men went about their jobs. He felt a tinge of excitement being back on the bridge of a warship, realizing he had a bit of admiration for this privately owned pirate navy. As much as he detested Escandoza and what he stood for, the drug lord definitely knew how to put together an elite military force.

The electronics officer watched the frequency scanner readout. "The *Carupano* is four thousand yards off our port bow."

"Good." Schafer pressed the intercom. "Sonar, Conn."

"Conn, sonar, aye."

"Contacts?"

"Still just the one, sir."

"All right, bring us to periscope depth."

"Aye, sir," came a reply from the first officer. "Periscope depth."

"What is the *Carupano*?" Skyler asked.

"Our ticket home, Mr. Knebel. The Americans will be searching for a submarine racing at full steam across the Atlantic. What they won't be looking for is an old Panamanian freighter plowing a labored course for South America."

"I don't understand," Skyler said.

"I intend to bring the *Tiger Shark* up under the *Carupano* close enough to turn our combined sonar signature into a single blip as we ride piggyback to Colombia." He emphasized by placing one palm of his hand over the other.

"Brilliant," Skyler said, realizing that if Schafer could pull this off, there was a good chance the korium would make it to Escandoza. Now he must decide—sabotage the sub, stop the shipment, and in effect commit suicide, or let it complete its journey and take his chances confronting Escandoza head-on.

"Search periscope up," Schafer ordered. The shiny tube rose into position and the captain pulled the focusing handles down making a rapid 360-degree sweep. "Dark skies, raining hard, not much to see." He turned to Skyler. "A nasty day to be on the surface." Schafer folded the handles. "Down scope." As the mechanism lowered with a whoosh, he returned to his chair. "Take us to within a thousand yards."

"Aye, sir," said the first officer. "One thousand yards."

Skyler watched as the helmsman adjusted his controls.

A few moments later the first officer called out, "One thousand yards, sir."

"Up periscope," Schafer ordered. Again, he unfolded the handles, making a quick sweep of the horizon. "There she is." He pulled away from the eyepiece. "Video."

Skyler and the first officer watched a large video monitor that was mounted above the plotting table as it blinked to life. A fuzzy black and white image appeared showing a turbulent sea covered with whitecaps. The *Carupano* was little more than a blurry form on the horizon, dark smoke flowing from its funnel.

"We have found our ride home, gentlemen." Schafer grinned proudly. He turned back to the eyepiece making one last sweep of the horizon.

Skyler watched the video monitor as the gray ocean rolled by. "Captain, what was that? You passed something, a small object."

Schafer seemed a bit annoyed as he panned the scope back in the opposite direction. "I see nothing."

"There *is* something," the first officer said. He took a step toward the screen and pointed.

Skyler watched as a bobbing, cone-shaped object came into focus.

"It's probably nothing more than a piece of flotsam discarded from the *Carupano*," the first officer said.

Schafer looked over at the video monitor then back through the scope. Suddenly he backed away, his mouth gaping. "Mother of God. It's a—"

"A sonobuoy," Skyler whispered.

"A goddamn sonobuoy!" the captain yelled.

"Captain!" screamed the electronics officer. "It just went active transmitting a burst on the Juliet-band!"

Schafer slammed the handles of the periscope closed. "Down scope! Crash dive!" His face paled as he turned to Skyler. "We're fucked!"

RUN DEEP

The USS *Orlando* cruised 200 feet below the surface, 300 miles northeast of Norfolk. Behind it, like bait on a fishing line trawling for game fish, it towed its fully optimized passive sonar arrays.

The skipper of the Los Angeles-class attack submarine was Commander Michael Webster, a broad shouldered former defensive back for the University of Alabama Crimson Tide. Webster sat in his captain's chair letting the soft hum of electronics in the sub's command center relax him. He closed his eyes, picturing his wife and newborn son and wanted more than anything to hold them both.

"Conn, sonar!"

The thin voice from the intercom brought Webster out of his meditation. "Conn, aye. Captain speaking."

"Contact, sir. Bearing two-three-zero."

"Range?" Webster asked.

"Approximately twenty-five thousand yards, Captain. Sonobuoy just popped its top."

"Can you identify?"

"From the plant signature I make it a Yankee-class boomer."

Damn if we didn't find him right out of the box, Commander Webster thought. "Thank you, Chief." He rose and called out, "Man battle stations." As alarms sounded, Webster said, "Helm, ahead two thirds. Bring us around to two-three-zero." Adrenaline rushed through him. "Weapons, put forty-eights in tubes one and two, and plot a solution." The commander watched the data input readout on his display monitor while he felt his ship turn toward the distant target.

"Coming around to new course two-three-zero, sir," called the helmsman.

"All stop," said Webster a moment later when the course was confirmed.

"Aye, sir, all stop," replied the helmsman.

"Weapons, flood tubes one and two."

A few seconds later the weapons officer acknowledged, "Tubes one and two are flooded, sir."

"Weapons, open outer doors one and two."

A pause, and then, "Doors one and two open, Captain."

"Do you have a solution yet?"

"Solution is confirmed, sir."

"Fire one and two!"

A burst of compressed-gas ejected the nineteen-foot-long, wire-guided Mark 48 torpedo from tube number one in the bow of the *Orlando*. As its five-hundred-horsepower engine spun to life, the torpedo accelerated. Like a newborn reluctant to detach its umbilical cord from its mother, the Mark 48 reeled out a wire from its tail and took a course twelve degrees off its intercept path. A few seconds later, a second Mark 48 emerged from tube number two. It sprang forward adjusting its course twelve degrees in the opposite direction so both torpedoes could cover the entire one hundred eighty-degree target sector. Carrying 650-pound warheads, the Mark 48s raced through the water at just over fifty miles-per-hour.

"Time to impact?" Webster asked, returning to his chair.

"Seventeen minutes, twenty seconds, sir," came the reply from Weapons.

"Let me know when you have acquisition." Webster let a smile cross his face. "Roll Tide," he whispered.

~~~

"High-speed screws, sir!" yelled the sonar operator over the intercom on the bridge of the *Tiger Shark*. "Torpedoes in the water!"

Skyler held on to the back of the captain's chair as the deck pitched forward in the crash dive. He saw the helmsman push the yoke to the hilt, exerting the maximum down position on the dive planes.

"Execute counter measures," Schafer ordered.

His voice lacked the confidence Skyler expected from a missile sub commander. As he studied the man, he felt a bump from the compressed-air modules being launched out of the sides of the vessel. Clouds of noisy bubbles would shoot out of each, the resulting racket designed to distract the incoming torpedoes and draw them away from their real target.

"Sonar, start jamming," Schafer said.

In the sonar control room, the operator attempted to create ghost targets by sending out timed pulses to coincide with the seeking pulses of the approaching torpedoes. He watched the data readouts then pressed the intercom. "Conn, sonar. The fish have not acquired us yet but are still running true."

Skyler watched Schafer grow nervous, figuring this may be the captain's first shot at commanding a boomer. As impressive as the crew was under the circumstances, it was still nothing more than a rag-tag band assembled by Escandoza from military organizations all over the world. Their lack of experience could prove deadly. Schafer's forehead glistened with sweat. He held on to the railing around the periscope pedestal. "I promised you entertainment," he said to Skyler. "I hope you're not disappointed."

Suddenly the bridge vibrated with a high-pitched metallic sound. *Ping . . .ping . . . ping . . .*

"They've acquired us!" the sonar operator blared over the intercom. The tremble in his voice was not lost on Skyler.

Two miles behind the *Tiger Shark*, the lead Mark 48 released its guidance wire as it acquired its target. Following ninety-one meters behind it, the second Mark 48 did the same. Calculating the distance to the enemy sub, they cut their speed by a third to conserve fuel and executed a series of minor course corrections.

Schafer moved to stand in front of Skyler. "Since we only have a few moments to live, *Mr. Skyler*, I thought we might be honest with each other."

"My picture on the news?" Skyler tried to remain unmoved at the discovery of his true identity.

"I've followed your accomplishments with interest as director of OceanQuest. You have a memorable face. My compliments to you for your quick thinking after you eliminated Knebel." Schafer wiped his forehead on his sleeve.

"Your first time in combat?"

"A first for many things. Too bad we don't get a second chance to die." Then his expression turned desperate.

"Captain," called the OOD. "The counter measures aren't working. The fish are still on track. Should I inform the *Carupano?*"

Schafer's eyes grew wide. He spun around facing the officer of the deck. "My God, I forgot about the freighter. Up planes!" he yelled. "Helmsman, put us on the deck as close to the *Carupano* as possible. Scrape the paint off her sides if you have to." Then he turned back to Skyler. "Maybe we do get a second chance."

~~~

Captain Sampson strolled out of the wheelhouse onto the wing of the *Carupano's* bridge and studied the next squall line approaching from the south. He watched the swells break against the bow shooting wings of spray up and over the rail. The spray stung his face and the wind whipped his oilskin jacket. He stared aft, sighting the riggings and hatches along the length of the 142-foot freighter. They seemed to be holding.

Suddenly, the sea off his starboard side appeared to boil. A massive dome of white foam blossomed up with such force, it caused the *Carupano* to list slightly to port. Captain Sampson stared with gaping mouth as the immense bullet-shaped bow of a submarine emerged from the midst of the foaming ocean. It seemed to rise up like a slow-motion rocket launched from the depths. For a moment, Sampson believed it would keep rising until it took flight. As he gripped the railing with white-knuckled hands, he watched the giant monster hang suspended, its bow exposed back to the sub's conning tower.

When the submarine reached its apex, it dropped forward sending up a sheet of spray that reached higher than the top of the bridge where Sampson stood. The wave slammed him against the steel wall forcing what felt like gallons of choking salt water down his throat.

Sampson fell to the deck, his big body trembled. As he pulled himself back to the railing, he witnessed the slippery, eel-like skin of the submarine reveal its full length. Just as soon as it had settled into the water, it lunged forward past him. He could not believe its speed and maneuverability when it pushed through the swells cutting across his path and missing his ship by a few scant yards.

The sea frothed with the swirling brass blades of the sub's twin screws as they cleared his bow. Sampson felt a sigh of relief escape his throat when he realized that as close as the sub had come, it had somehow managed to miss his ship. He gave a nervous laugh at how two enormous vessels could find each other in the middle of an empty ocean, come so close to disaster, and get away without a scratch.

All laughter died with his next breath, and his guts wrenched as the stern of the *Carupano* lifted out of the water several feet and then dropped back onto the ocean with a crippling concussion. Sampson watched a huge fireball form over the aft deck with a force that peeled the deck back like a sardine can.

The ship shuddered, its modest forward motion dying almost immediately. Black smoke rose up in a thick column with an acid stench assaulting the captain's nostrils. The heat singed his hair and he covered his eyes as the blast enveloped half his ship.

Sampson found himself on his back, the smell of burnt flesh causing bile to rise in his throat. He pulled himself to a sitting position, looking at the mass of wreckage that used to be his ship.

The captain reached for the railing trying to stand when the second Mark 48 plowed its warhead into the hapless side of the ship. It struck just below the waterline only thirty feet from where he stood. In the next instant the paint on the bridge boiled, the steel deck turned to liquid, and Captain Sampson ceased to exist.

THE RIM

Communist Party Headquarters, Pyongyang, North Korea

The city plunged into darkness as the air raid sirens wailed. Lights from government buildings and apartments, streetlights, businesses, and automobile headlights were extinguished during the weekly, ten-minute drill. The General Secretary watched from his office window as giant monolithic structures across the sprawling capital disappeared into a black landscape of non-descript shapes.

"What a waste of time," he said while closing the thick drapes. He turned to face General Cho. "Anyone who watches CNN knows the enemy needs no city lights to target their smart bombs and cruise missiles."

"A true observation, Beloved Leader." Cho stood stiffly waiting for the General Secretary to return to his desk. "But it gives our comrade citizens a feeling of security to know we are concerned enough for their safety to conduct such exercises."

"All it accomplishes is to justify the existence of some of the military dinosaurs that still populate the leadership of the Peoples Army." The General Secretary sat and rubbed his face with a sense of frustration. "This whole thing has dragged on too long. Mistakes and dependency on pirates and outlaws is all we seem to be able to accomplish. Can the schedule be pushed up?"

"The timing must be precise, Beloved Leader. Taking over the lab too soon may cost us delays later if the Candles are not completed. Moving too late will mean we are at a disadvantage in dealing with Escandoza. I must bring our troops in at just the right moment."

"Yes, I'm sure you're right." The General Secretary leaned back and gazed into space. "All preparations are complete in Panama?"

"The freighter *Sunan* has made the Canal passage many times—it is a legitimate grain hauler. There will be no inspections, no search. Its papers have been cleared in advance. I have made a number of people very wealthy to guarantee it."

"The Americans did us a favor giving the Canal back to the greedy Panamanians." He chuckled at the thought. Then he stood and walked around the desk. "You have done well, General. Once we bring our enemies to their knees and unite our two countries into one great nation, I have special plans for you as a reward for your loyal service."

Chol bowed. "I am unworthy of your praise, Beloved Leader."

"Go and command our troops to the first of many glorious victories. I only wish I could be there to see you lead our elite commandos when they descend upon the Colombians."

~~~

"We're losing light," Candice Stevens said. "Another five minutes and we call it quits." She planted her hiking boots firmly in the dirt—her khaki shorts and bushman shirt were a few shades darker than the surrounding terrain. To her side, the bank of strobes flashed a dozen times in rapid succession as she aimed the Nikon.

The Navajo model, a seventeen-year-old girl with midnight black hair, moved with grace against the backdrop of the setting Arizona sun. She posed a few yards from the rim of Meteor Crater—a mile-wide, bowl-shaped hole that formed twenty-two thousand years before when a giant nickel-iron ball crashed into the earth. The bleak landscape formed by the collision contrasted to the vibrant colors of the traditional Indian costume the girl wore for the *American West* photo shoot.

"That's a rap," Candice announced. She handed her camera to her assistant, a tall, black man named Carl. He removed the digital memory card as Candice walked over to the girl. "You were excellent."

"You really think so?" She beamed.

"Absolutely." Candice gave her a business card. "As a matter of fact, I'm going to have my agent get in touch with you. I can't guarantee anything, but a mix of natural talent and beauty like yours are hard to find. I feel certain she'll be able to get you additional shoots. You have a portfolio and up-to-date head shots?"

The young Navajo nodded.

"Have them ready for her." Candice gave her a smile and thank-you hug. Then she walked over to the grip, a burly man in his late forties with a heavy red beard. "Nice job as always, Mike."

"Thanks, Candy." He was busy loosening the brackets holding the strobes and reflectors to the lighting tripods.

Candice went to her silver Grand Cherokee and opened a backpack resting on the front passenger's seat. Pulling out a cloth, she wiped the dust from her forehead. Then she took a long drink from a bottle of spring water. It was the fourth bottle today—the desert dried her out like an autumn leaf, she thought, while she searched for hand lotion. She took one last look at a clipboard listing the shoot schedule to make sure she had not missed a shot. The magazine was on a shoestring budget—they could not even afford a makeup artist. Candice had performed that task in addition to taking the pictures. Placing the clipboard down, she turned to enjoy the last of the blazing sunset, reminiscent of a Joseph Turner masterpiece she and Matt had enjoyed in London's Tate Gallery. There was a formation of boulders about fifty yards to the north. She strolled over and sat on one near the crater rim while the crew packed up.

Candice thought of Skyler. She had not heard from him in over a week. There had been the call from the *Phoenix* right after Matt had arrived in Greenland, and the one short message telling her they had found the cargo plane under the ice. Then nothing. But this was not unusual. After all, Matt was an explorer of the first order—his job took him to the farthest corners of the globe. She was used to not hearing from him for extended periods of time. But he had promised to let her know just as soon as he left Greenland. At that point, the job should be over, he had told her. They planned to meet in Key West and get away for a few days, maybe to some secluded cay in the Bahamas. She should have heard something by now. She would give him hell for not calling, she thought—just before she took him to heaven.

Candice was distracted from her thoughts by the crunch of tires on the gravel access road leading up from

Interstate 40. Approaching headlights danced in the twilight—the sound of a truck engine drifted on the light desert wind.

A Chevy SUV pulled beside Mike's lighting truck. Candice could just make out Arizona State Police on the fender. The last rays of the setting sun reflected off the red and blue emergency lights.

Two uniformed men got out. Voices carried across the parched landscape as Mike and Carl conferred with the troopers. While the Navajo girl stood nearby, the troopers appeared to question the two men. Then Mike raised his arm, pointing in the direction of the boulders where Candice sat.

It must be about renewing that stupid permit from the state film commission, Candice thought. She started to get up when flashes lit up the scene. At first, Candice thought Mike's strobes went off. Then she clamped her hand over her mouth to muffle her scream as the two troopers gunned down Carl and Mike. The Indian girl turned and ran through the beams of the SUV's headlights. Her screams of terror echoed off the rocks. A second later, her arms flew up, her back arched, and she collapsed face down from bullets slamming into her back. One of the troopers stood over her while the second, pistol in hand, turned in Candice's direction.

With her sandy-colored clothes blending into the twilight surroundings, Candice slipped off the boulder and moved through the darkness along the rim of the crater. She felt her heart race as blood roared in her ears, her breaths coming in shallow gasps. "Don't panic," she whispered repeatedly. She felt her way along the wall of rocks daring not to look to her side—the steep rim of the crater was only a few steps away.

Crouching beside a large rock, she strained to see her pursuer. His dark form moved across the distance directly toward her, a strange black object covered his face.

How can he see so well in the dark? she thought. Then she knew—Night vision goggles!

Realizing the rocks offered little concealment, Candice leaped to her feet and ran at a sprint along the rim of the crater. Her eyes blurred with tears. She felt her feet slip on the loose gravel—her arms extended to keep from smashing into a hidden wall of rock.

Above the sound of her desperate footfalls came the grunting of someone running hard behind her—and he was gaining. She could hear his breathing—feel his presence, his strength.

His hand grazed her back grabbing at her shirt. A sound came from deep in her throat—one she had never heard before—the cry of the fleeing gazelle being overtaken by the lion. Then he was on her, clawing at her clothes, spinning her, wrapping his powerful arms around her. Their momentum carried them a dozen yards farther before Candice hit the ground hard—hot pain shooting through her shoulder.

He was at her feet scrambling to rise and pin her down. Kicking wildly, Candice rolled out of his grip—pushing, fighting, and managing to stand. He lunged and her legs went out from under her. Next there was blackness as she tumbled over the rim.

THE PLAN

United States Southern Command Headquarters, Miami

Gates gazed down at the horizontal LED display monitor. It showed a three-dimensional, computer-generated representation of Lake Guatavita and the surrounding mountains thirty kilometers north of Bogotá. The image was complete with texture mapping of the lake's rugged shoreline along with the dense jungle that covered the land leading up to the Andes foothills. A small village and a few farms dotted the rolling hills bordering the lake. There was enough detail for Gates to count cattle in a pasture. He used the joystick console control to rotate the image so he could examine it from every angle. An electronic grid displayed elevations, distances and water depth at various points across the lake.

"What are those buildings?" Gates asked. He pointed to a group of two-story structures nestled a few hundred meters up a long, steep valley about a kilometer from the north end of the lake.

"An exclusive mountain resort," said Colonel Argentine. "It's a retreat for Escandoza's top management. They periodically hold business conferences, entertain politicians, government officials, and others on the drug lord's payroll. It's also the entrance to the Keep, his underground private residence."

"And that's where the lab is? Underground?" Gates asked.

"We think so," said Lieutenant Elaine Coffee, a slim brunette from the computer analysis division of the Air Force Special Anti-terrorism Unit. She leaned over the display and gestured to a steep rock wall overhanging a portion of the resort. "If you look closely you can see a number of small structures along the upper edge of the cliff. Those are ventilation and exhaust ducts."

"He's picked a perfect location," Gates said. "There's only one way in—only one direction to defend."

"Exactly," Argentine said. "Up the valley from the lake."

"Approaching from the higher elevations would be next to impossible even for an expert climbing team," said Coffee. "The mountains get more rugged the higher you go. The valley walls are equally out of the question as an approach route."

"Our operatives in the region tell us the place is protected with the latest infrared imaging along with motion and heat sensors," Argentine said. "We believe there's also a significant amount of munitions and antipersonnel devices hidden within the surrounding jungle." He turned as the door opened to the dimly-lit intelligence-gathering control room.

Gates looked up to see the entrance fill with the massive silhouette of a man who could easily be a member of the NFL. As he stepped into the room, Gates guessed his weight at over 250lbs and height at an inch below the door frame. Even with the enormous size, Gates noticed that he walked more with the agility of a quarterback than a lineman.

"Come in, Captain," Argentine said. "I'd like you to meet Mr. Mickey Gates, Projects Director for OceanQuest and our primary adviser on this mission." Argentine turned to Gates. "This is Captain Gordon Rees, commander of the Army Rangers Rapid Response Team."

As a former U.S. Olympic wrestling champion, Gates rarely found a person's handshake impressive or his equal for that matter. But he hid a slight grimace as Rees' viselike grip encased the marine explorer's hand. "Nice to meet you," Gates said with a dry smile.

The black officer nodded as Argentine motioned them all to a conference table.

When they were seated, Gates said, "What about the ventilation shafts? Can you use them to gain access?"

"We don't have enough information," Coffee said.

"So do you have a plan?" Gates asked Argentine.

"Captain Rees and his Rangers have been rehearsing the assault for the last two weeks."

"Our first priority is to locate and disable the electrical systems," said Rees.

"Does Escandoza have generators?" Gates asked.

"There's power running to the Keep from a substation near the lake," Coffee said. "We have to assume he has backup generators. We just haven't confirmed it yet."

"Why not go in with the heavy stuff?" Gates said. "Forget the ground assault. Slip a few laser-guided party favors through the front door."

"Won't work," Argentine said. "The Colombian Air Force is small but highly trained and well equipped.

Because they are sympathetic to and partially funded by Escandoza, their resistance presents too big a risk."

"It has to be a small assault team," Rees said. "One that can get in quickly and destroy the lab."

"So what do you need from me?" Gates asked.

"You know the area around the lake well, correct?" Rees said.

"The Colombian Department of Antiquities contracted us to dive for artifacts in the lake about ten years ago. I spent three months in the area. But back then, there was no resort, no fortress."

"Doesn't matter," Argentine said. "If you can assist Captain Rees in analyzing the best entrance and exit routes, it would save us a lot of guesswork, possibly even lives."

"How about I go with you?" Gates said.

"Out of the question," Rees said. "My men are trained professionals—experts at assault and insertion. You're a marine salvager, a good one no doubt, but a civilian. And this is no place for a civilian."

Gates stiffened. "Suit yourself, Captain. But my best friend is somewhere out in the middle of the Atlantic on an enemy submarine heading right into the middle of this mess. I intend to move those mountains if necessary to get him out. And if you don't want me to join your little shindig, then I'll just form one of my own and take care of the problem myself. While you're fumbling around in the jungle, I'll be closing up shop for Mr. Escandoza and bringing Matt Skyler home."

Rees glared at Gates, his eyelids narrowing.

"So what'll it be?" Gates said. "All of me or none at all?"

After an uneasy pause, Argentine said, "Gentlemen, I think some compromise can be reached here." He looked at Rees. "Captain, how about if Mr. Gates goes in as far as the lake, gets you within striking distance, and then lays back while your men finish their job?"

Before Rees could answer, Gates said, "I'll be glad to hold the Captain's hand until he's standing on old Pablo's doorstep."

Rees never took his eyes off Gates. "The second I think you're jeopardizing my men, your all-expense-paid vacation to South America will be terminated. I don't care if you're former Navy and some big international hero. In my world you're just another JQ Public."

"That's Mr. JQ to you," Gates said with a grin.

SHARK ATTACK

"Direct hit, sir," said the sonar operator on the *Orlando*. He pressed his earphones against his head, his eyes closed with a look of deep concentration. Ten seconds later, he said, "Impact number two. Confirming catastrophic damage. Bulkheads collapsing and secondary explosions."

"Good work, Sonar," Commander Webster said, beaming. He stood and turned to the OOD. "Slow to one third. Prepare to surface."

"Aye, sir," the officer of the deck replied. "Should I notify COMSUBLANT?"

"I want a visual confirm first," Webster said. "Then you can fire off the good news to the boss." His chest swelled as he looked around the command center. "Fine job, gentlemen and ladies. I can assure you that—"

"Conn, Sonar." The seaman's voice blared over the intercom. "Torpedo in the water. Bearing two-one-zero."

Webster stared up at the speaker box. "What did you say?"

"Holy shit!" the sonar operator shouted. "Conn, Sonar, we've got multiple torpedoes in the water."

"Sonar, this is the captain. Who the hell's shooting at us?"

"It's the sub, sir," the sonar operator said. "They're still alive. We must have hit another vessel."

Webster turned to his OOD. "Execute counter measures!"

"Aye, sir." The officer of the deck repeated the command.

"Conn, Sonar. One of the torpedoes has gone to active pings."

"What's the range?" Webster knew the distance could be estimated by the intervals between pings.

"Conn, Sonar. It's continuous."

Webster exchanged grave looks with the OOD, realizing a continuous ping meant the torpedoes were so close that their guidance systems had a precise fix on their target. He had only one chance to save his boat. "Emergency blow, fore and aft!" he shouted. "Twenty degree up-bubble. Chief, get us on the deck!"

"Aye, sir." The chief of the watch grabbed the intercom mic. "Emergency blow. Surface! Surface! Surface!" Around him, bells clamored and sirens wailed.

Webster hoped he could get above the upper threshold setting of the torpedoes and force them to detonate their warheads at the false targets created by the tremendous exhaust of bubbles. At worst, even if his sub took a hit, he would be on the surface—a better chance of saving his men.

With a loud shriek, high-pressurized air shot into the ballast tanks forcing the seawater out and making the sub lighter. Webster grasped the railing as the deck pitched up.

He could see the speed indicator—they were shooting toward the surface at forty-two knots.

Over the noise of the alarms, Webster heard the approaching torpedo's continuous sonar pinging. And mixed with it was the high-pitched, power-drill scream of the weapon's screws—now at full throttle.

"Brace for impact!" Webster yelled.

It came like a crack of thunder. The first torpedo ripped the hull open just beneath the turbine generators. Water rushed in filling the surrounding compartments and killing dozens of seamen. The second struck below the reactor compartment. It tore apart the steam generator and cooling pipes. Seawater flooded through the gaping holes and slowed the sub's frantic assent to a crawl.

The command center went dark as screams mixed with the sound of ripping steel. Dense smoke filled the air causing Webster to cough and gag. He heard the roar of seawater slamming through the compartments behind him and he cursed as a large piece of equipment, probably a plotting table, struck him in the chest, pinning him against the wall. He made an effort to push against it as tons of water crashed into him.

The submarine split and spilled its contents out of the jagged wounds as it fell into the black abyss. Moments later, the first fragments came to rest on the ocean floor not more than 400 meters from the debris field of the *Carupano*.

As the wreckage from the *Orlando* settled onto the sandy bottom, the sound of the *Tiger Shark* faded into the vast expanse of ocean.

ISLAND OF BLOOD

After refueling at a secluded airfield outside Caracas, the small, unmarked cargo plane transported Captain Rees and his Rangers along with Gates across the Venezuelan border into Colombia. Skirting the eastern foothills of the Andes, the plane landed on an abandoned jungle airstrip ten kilometers north of Lake Guatavita near the small town of Sesquile.

Dressed in camouflage and using night-vision goggles, Gates and the ten-man Ranger infiltration team slipped silently through the thick forest. They avoided the few remote farms and villages along the trail leading to the lake.

Gates wondered if the real enemy was the jungle itself. Waves of insects, like tiny kamikaze pilots, buzzed around him as the group moved through the night under a moonless sky. Maintaining a steady pace, the men rarely paused to rest.

Amplified by his night-vision goggles, the jungle took on a strange alien-like appearance. Gates remembered what he didn't like about this place from the last time he was here ten years ago searching for Indian artifacts. The days were hot, the nights heavy and oppressive, and the bugs were everywhere. Welcome back, he thought, feeling the sweat forming rivulets down his spine.

He wondered about Skyler. Was he still on the sub or somewhere in Colombia? Maybe even already at The Keep? He would do anything to help him—a friend he treasured with his own life. He tried not to think of the worst.

Gates watched Rees and the small group move silently along the jungle path. Even though they had butted heads at the start, Rees was obviously a professional with only one thing on his mind—the success of the mission. Although Rees kept a watchful eye on Gates, little was said between them since the mission started. Rees'orders to everyone were straightforward and clear-cut. His team members displayed a genuine respect for the captain and carried out his commands without hesitation. They were trained well and eager for action.

The soldier in the lead held up his arm and formed a tight fist. The group froze, their weapons ready. Then the soldier flicked on a small spotlight and aimed it at a point a few dozen meters ahead. Its beam reflected back two laser-red dots. Gates held his breath, waiting. But it took only an instant for the predator to realize it was outmatched. With a blink, the two dots disappeared as the jaguar bounded away into the night.

Giving the big cat a moment to distance itself, the lead soldier made a quick gesture and the group moved on. Gates knew that predators of the four-legged kind would be the least of their problems.

It was just past midnight when they came to the valley entrance leading to The Keep.

~~~

General Cho stood on the bridge of the *Sunan* as the freighter passed through the Cristobal breakwater. He watched Limon Bay disappear into the setting sun. They had made the nine-hour journey through the Panama Canal without attracting attention. The harbor pilot had received $10,000 in advance to ask no questions.

As the sky darkened, the General watched his commando unit emerge from below. They wandered out onto the decks to take in the fresh sea air, after being cooped up in secret cargo compartments since the ship approached the western coast of Panama. Soon, they would start their final preparation for the assault on the lab. Before heading below decks for dinner, the General glanced up into the star-filled sky one last time.

Four hundred kilometers overhead the photo surveillance satellite aimed its infrared high-resolution camera and recorded a series of digital images. A few seconds later, the Korean general's face appeared on a video monitor in the image analysis section of the National Security Agency in Fort Meade, Maryland.

~~~

"Pablo Escandoza has declared war on the United States," Buck Stone said.

The President looked at the Secretary of Defense and then around the conference table at the directors of the DoD, CIA, NSA, and FBI, their assistants, and General Mitchell Greer, Chairman of the Joint Chiefs. The two-dozen members of the National Crisis Team met deep below the main levels of the White House in the Crisis Command Center.

"How many were on the *Orlando*?" the President asked.

"One hundred and twenty-nine including thirteen officers," Stone replied.

"Survivors?"

Stone stared back with a bleak expression.

The Secretary of the Navy glanced up from his notes before continuing to write on a legal pad. "A second vessel was also destroyed," said Lancaster.

"We believe it was a commercial vessel of some sort, not military," Stone said.

"Where is the sub now, Tom?"

"Mr. President," Lancaster said, "I'm afraid we've lost the target."

The President removed his wire-rimmed glasses and rubbed his eyes. "This has gone way beyond a simple matter of dealing with a Colombian drug lord and his cocaine smuggling operation. We've lost the lives of over a hundred patriots and one of our most advanced warships. National security is at stake. Appropriate action must be taken."

"Mr. President," White House Chief of Staff, Nathan Templeton said. "Before any firm decisions are made, we must address the question of the North Korean involvement." He nodded to Allen Grant.

A wall-mounted video monitor displayed an overhead view of a ship underway in the open waters of the Caribbean. The President could see a few dozen men standing around an exposed area of the ship's forward deck.

The director of the CIA pointed a remote control at the monitor and the image changed to a fuzzy shot of a man's face looking up into the camera. "That is General Cho Dal-Yun," Grant said. "General Cho commands the First Shock Army of North Korea. He is also personal confidant and adviser to the General Secretary. Cho is the primary contact between the General Secretary and Pablo Escandoza."

Grant aimed the remote again and the monitor changed to an infrared image of the ship. The enhanced photo showed figures of the men on the deck.

"When was this taken, Allen?" The President saw that they all wore military uniforms and carried weapons.

"Six hours ago, Mr. President. The vessel is the *Sunan*, a freighter registered in Thailand to a shipping company with strong connections to North Korea. The *Sunan* passed through the Panama Canal just before sunset and headed north into the Caribbean Sea."

"Away from Colombia?"

"Yes, sir," Grant said.

"That doesn't make sense."

"It does, sir, if they've moved the korium lab to someplace offshore," said Buck Stone.

"Any predictions on its next port of call?" the President asked.

"Nothing definite," Grant said and clicked the remote again. A map appeared showing a series of islands in the shape of a crescent moon. "But we can assume that if Escandoza has moved the lab, it would be to someplace remote—an island with little or no population or shipping traffic. The best choice is this archipelago lying about 700 kilometers northwest of the Colombian mainland. It happens to be Colombia's territory and is made up of two main groups of islands. The southern one is the largest and is called Isla de San Andres. And the northern one is Isla de Providencia. There are several other islands in the group scattered over a large area. Most are volcanic in origin and are covered with mountains, thick rain forests, and rocky beaches. They've supported inhabitants down through the centuries but most are currently unpopulated. We believe one of them is the destination of the *Sunan* and the possible location of the korium lab."

"Why do you think they would move the lab?"

"Probably to throw off the Koreans, Mr. President," Grant said. "Looks like it didn't work."

"Plus," Thomas Lancaster added, "they need a place to dock the sub and unload the korium. A place that's isolated, private, and almost invisible."

The President tapped a pencil on his notepad. "Is the *Nimitz* and her support group still off the North Korean coast?"

"No, sir," Lancaster said. "She moved off station three days ago."

"Then turn her around. Bring her back. Start some maneuvers to send an obvious signal to North Korea. If they want trouble, we'll be glad to oblige. In the meantime, aim every surveillance resource we've got at that island. If a coconut drops, I want to know before it hits the ground. And this matter of the Korean freighter with Cho on board. Alert the Fourth Fleet commander. Have his closest warships steam at full speed to intercept the *Sunan*. Stop and board. If they resist, put her on the bottom."

"North Korea will raise holy hell, sir," Grant said.

"Do I look like I care?"

"What about informing our allies, sir?" Templeton asked.

"Let them know we intend to take appropriate action to put a stop to this madman." The President turned to General Mitchell Greer. "What about the insertion team?"

"Yes, sir. They're on the ground now—their last report stated that they had made entry into the underground portion of Escandoza's stronghold and found it deserted. No personnel and no lab equipment. Looks like the drug lord and the technicians made a quick exit. We have to assume they were tipped off."

"Or they had already planned on moving long before we got there."

Greer nodded.

"The OceanQuest man? The one that liked beer. He's with them?"

"Yes, sir."

"And what about Matt Skyler?"

"Still no word, sir," Greer said.

He turned to Grant. "Allen, which one of the islands would you pick as the best choice for the lab?"

"This one, sir." Grant aimed a laser pointer at the map.

"Contact the insertion team immediately. Fill them in on the latest intelligence. Get them a fast extraction and point them in the direction of that island." As everyone started to rise, he asked, "What is it called?"

"Isla de Sangre, sir—Island of Blood."

LEAP OF FAITH

It was just after 7:00 PM when Skyler felt the forward motion of the *Tiger Shark* slow and finally cease. Soon, the ever-present hum of the steam turbine engines driven by the nuclear power plant went silent. He sat in the small captain's dining room waiting to be summoned to his fate as he listened to crew members moving about in the hallway beyond. The harrowing experience of dodging two Mark 48's had left him and the rest of the crew shaken. He also felt that Schafer, although lacking experience as a boomer commander, showed quick thinking and courage in getting through the ordeal. And Skyler got the impression that the captain's loyalty to Escandoza would last only as long as the money flowed. Could he convince Schafer that it was imperative to stop the drug lord and avoid a possible mass killing? Would he even get the chance?

Key's jingled in the lock and the door opened. Two sailors stood outside—one motioned for Skyler to rise and follow. Both were armed with assault rifles. As he got to the door, he realized that Captain Schafer was there as well. Like the captain, the crew all wore naval-style uniforms. But there were no markings that identified what navy or the allegiance to any particular country. Still, it was smart on Schafer's part, Skyler thought, to make his pirates wear uniforms—it brought them together as a team, however ragtag it might be.

"Should we restrain him, Captain?" one of the sailors asked.

Schafer chuckled. "Where's he going to go?" Then he motioned to Skyler. "This way. And try not to hijack my boat. We're docked."

Skyler followed the captain along the corridor with the sailors in tow. Soon they arrived at the base of a ladder leading to an open hatch. Skyler saw a star-filled sky—the last hues of twilight fading. The captain started climbing. He paused long enough to motion that Skyler follow. Seconds later, they stood on the deck of the *Tiger Shark*. It was then that Skyler realized how big a vessel it was. Most obvious to where he stood were the twelve hatch covers protecting the SS-N-17 Snipe SLBM's. For a moment he felt as if he stood on a powder keg with the fuse about to be lit.

"Welcome to Isla de Sangre."

"Blood Island," Skyler said. "How appropriate."

"Don't be so pessimistic, Mr. Skyler. If you remain docile and non-threatening, you may actually survive this ordeal. And to be honest, because I like you, I hope you do."

"You're much too kind."

Schafer motioned to the submarine. "Impressive, isn't she?"

"I'll grant you that, Captain. For a boat built in the seventies, she's aged well. We should both be so lucky."

As they walked along the deck, Skyler took in his surroundings. The *Tiger Shark* had pulled alongside a heavy-planked wooden loading dock that stretched at least 200 meters from shore. He assumed it must have served as an industrial wharf sometime in the past. This would also account for the water depth allowing the sub to maneuver alongside. Based on his experience, he guessed the sub's draft to be around eight meters. Other ships, probably small freighters or fishing trawlers must have docked here, and needed that much clearance. This was consistent with the Cold Bay fishery docking arrangement. Forward hatches on the sub were already being opened in preparation for offloading the containers of korium.

The wharf led to a rocky shore, probably lava, Skyler thought. Beyond lay a number of buildings that could have been former seafood processing plants. He assumed they had been converted into the lab set up by Escandoza to refine the korium and build the Candles. A float plane sat tied up on the opposite side of the wharf. To the right of the dock and sub was a lagoon that Skyler estimated to be about one hundred meters wide. Barely visible in the gathering darkness was a strip of white beach leading to a thick grove of palms and a dark jungle beyond. Against the disappearing twilight he saw the outline of mountains.

It's now or never, Skyler thought. This was his only chance. He took two broad steps, sprung off the side of the sub and dove into the lagoon. Staying underwater, he swam as far as he could, hoping there were no coral reefs to tear his skin, and that his Naval Academy training would prove true in his stamina to hold his breath.

One of the sailors stepped up beside Schafer and aimed his assault rifle. "Should I stop him, Captain?"

Schafer waved him off. "We'll find him. It's a small island."

FOOT RACE

S kyler hit the sandy bottom in the shallows of the lagoon. He sprang to his feet and sprinted toward the protection of the coconut palms. Why weren't they shooting? he thought. Despite the darkness, he had to be a clear target against the white sand. Something was wrong. Schafer might be an OK guy, but not *that* OK.

He reached the first of the palms and pressed up against the back of a thick trunk. With caution, he peered around it in the direction of the sub. A series of floods lit the length of the wharf as the crew unloaded the ore containers. Schafer was walking toward the shore. Behind him, one of the armed sailors followed. Neither seemed at all concerned that their prisoner had just managed to escape. Then it occurred to him there was no reason for alarm because there was no chance of escaping the Island of Blood.

He slipped from behind the palm and made his way into the jungle. It was now pitch black and the thick canopy hid any starlight. His trek was slow going and painful— everything seemed to reach out and snag, trip, cut and sting. As he pushed his way through the thick vegetation, he wondered—if they weren't concerned with him escaping, that he would cause any trouble to the lab and their korium project. He would have to prove them wrong.

~~~

After a half hour of fighting through the jungle, Skyler maneuvered around to approach the buildings from the rear. Of the structures, only one was surrounded by a high, chain link fence—coiled razor wire ran along the top. Multiple floodlights lit the building. An armed guard with a Doberman on a leash walked along the side.

He watched the man's routine—it took roughly four minutes to complete the building's circumference. As the guard was about to disappear around a corner, Skyler shifted his weight causing his foot to come down on dry vegetation. The snap was loud enough for the Doberman to halt and point his nose at the source of the noise. The guard unclipped the leash and let the dog run. The only thing standing between Skyler and the charging animal was the fence.

Earlier, Skyler had seen what appeared to be a road leading away from the building into the jungle, and now he headed for it. Quickly, he was on the well-traveled dirt road and sprinting along with the help of starlight no longer blocked by the canopy. Judging by the barking, the dog was eager for action. Skyler knew it was only a matter of time before the guard would open a gate and release him. He had just a few minutes lead. That would vanish fast. At some point he would have to leave the road and return to the jungle. It would be slower going for him but also for the dog. He could tell by the sound the animal was now free of the fence and the foot race was on.

Shifting direction to the right, he was again immersed into the blackness of the jungle. The ground became uneven—the undergrowth whipped at him while he tried to keep his balance. Then for a second he realized something had changed. The barking. He froze and listened. Silence. Had he somehow thrown the dog off scent? Maybe the guard called the Doberman back? Or was the animal searching for the spot where Skyler reentered the jungle?

The latter became instantly confirmed. With what must have been a surge of adrenalin, the sound of the dog racing into the underbrush caused Skyler to turn and start running again. His theory that the dense growth would slow the dog was immediately shot down—he was close enough that Skyler heard his heavy breathing. Shouts from the guard were lost in the darkness.

Within seconds, the Doberman was at Skyler's heels. They were both breathing hard as they tore through the underbrush. Then came the bite—hard and vicious. The jaws latched on to his left boot at his ankle. With his next step, the ground fell away. He looked at the stars as he and the dog dropped into the void.

THE TEMPLE

Skyler floated on his back and studied the dark green canopy of the jungle fifteen meters over his head. The dawn tried to penetrate down into the ancient sacrificial well which he knew was called a cenote. The dim light revealed precious little of his prison. He could just make out the circular shape of the limestone walls, pitted and etched with age and erosion. He had managed to survive the night by climbing onto a small ledge sticking out from the wall. The dog had not been so lucky having struck the wall on the way down. It lived for only a half hour before sinking below the surface to join the bones of human and animal sacrifices from centuries before.

Ages ago, the naturally formed sinkhole accepted offerings to the gods that were believed to help bring rain, abundant crops, or victory against an enemy. Those that were tossed into its black depth never escaped—the sheer walls made sure of that. But the eons of abandonment, the cycles of flood and drought, and the unrelenting intrusion of the jungle made escape not easy, but at least possible. Thick vines and roots draped down the sides of the well in a snake-like tapestry. Combined with the pitted limestone, the plant-ropes would be Skyler's way out. With a mighty heave, he grabbed hold of the lowest hanging vine and pulled himself out of the rancid slime. Soon, he had worked his way to the lip of the cenote and crawled over the edge onto the jungle floor.

Skyler stood and took in his surroundings. If a search party had come looking for him, there was no sign of it. During the hours he lay on the ledge in the cenote, he heard nothing that would signal they were hunting him. Perhaps they believed he had followed the road further inland. Its gradual incline must lead to the mountains he spotted when he was taken from the sub. Although the jungle surrounded him, at his feet was the slightest hint of a stone path leading away from the sinkhole. He wondered how many victims stood on the last stone at the edge of the cenote before being thrown into the blackness.

He followed the partially overgrown stone path that zigzagged through thick vegetation. The incline became more noticeable, and at one point turned into steps. Then out of the emerald gloom, a structure appeared. A two-story temple covered in green moss. Vines and roots slowly strangled the ancient building in an eternal death grip. The temple blended into its surroundings like a ghost from a lost civilization.

There were four entrances across the front all leading to a single interior space, probably where the sacrificial victims were prepped for their final journey down the stone path. As Skyler approached one of the doorways, he heard a faint whimpering—his first thought was possibly an injured animal. He moved slowly into the dark interior but could see nothing. The sound came from a far corner and increased as he took one more step inside. It became a mixture of crying and muffled attempts to speak.

As he moved further into the room, he could just make out a human form huddled in a corner—hands and feet bound, a hood covered the head. He stood over the trembling body—a woman. Reaching, he pulled the hood away.

"Sweet Jesus! Candy!"

THE CAVALRY

Skyler removed the gag from Candice's mouth along with the ropes that bound her, and helped her to her feet. He took her into his arms.

"How did you get here?" he asked, then smothered her face with kissed.

"I thought I would never see you again, Sky." She returned his hugs and kisses. "They kidnapped me from my photo shoot in Arizona and flew me to someplace in the mountains of Colombia, then to here."

"Who are *they*?"

"His men. That drug lord. Escandoza."

"He's here on the island?"

"I am."

Skyler turned to see a silhouette framed in the narrow entrance to the temple. Behind him stood a female dressed in military camouflage and six armed guards.

"Welcome to Isla de Sangre, Mr. Skyler. I am your host, Pablo Escandoza. This is my corporate consultant, Teresa Castillo and a few of my loyal soldiers."

"What the hell's going on here," Skyler said. "Why did you kidnap Candice?"

Escandoza pointed a pistol at Skyler. "Ms. Stevens was to be my bait that at some point would draw you to me. I had hoped that you and I could negotiate an arrangement whereby you would work for my organization. You have proved very resourceful, and you could have been a great asset. If you had accepted my offer, then Ms. Stevens would go on taking beautiful pictures of beautiful models. That all changes now that I can no longer return to my Lake Guatavita headquarters thanks to your friend Gates and the Army Rangers."

"First I've heard of it. But if anyone can bring down the house, it would be Mick."

The drug lord laughed. "A loyal friend. Now you get to pay the price of his actions."

"So you hold a grudge?" Skyler maneuvered Candice to stand behind him.

Escandoza swept the hair from his eyes. "Someone must be punished. I've lost something dear to me, now you get to lose something, too. The sacred well is about to accept two more sacrifices. First, you get to watch Ms. Stevens die. Then you go next. Only this time, you won't be climbing out. With chains binding your ankles, you and your lady friend will join those going before you thousands of years ago. Better practice holding your breath." Escandoza spoke a command in Spanish. The guards moved into the ancient temple and took hold of Skyler and Candice. Their hands were bound behind them, then the men pushed them out of the temple toward the path to the cenote.

As he and Candice worked their way down the stone steps, Skyler said, "You realize it's only a matter of time before they find this island and the korium lab."

239

Escandoza and Castillo walked a few steps behind them while three guards led the group and three trailed behind. One held two pair of leg irons. "They may find this place, Mr. Skyler, but they will not attack. You see, there is one thing I haven't told you. My ace in the hole—isn't that what you Americans like to say? It will be a big surprise for your military and your country."

"And what is that?"

"An extra Candle. An assault on this island will result in the destruction of one of your major cities."

Skyler glanced at Candice. This was not good news. The lab was set up to manufacture additional Candles for sale to terrorists around the globe. But because of the lack of korium before finding the Arctic Air Cargo shipment, he never anticipated there was an additional device already in existence. Escandoza was right. If he threated the U.S. with an attack, the President would never risk a loss of life. There would have to be a different way to stop this madman.

Skyler saw the rim of the cenote come into view. Seconds later, he and Candice stood at the lip of the sacrificial well.

"I'm sorry it must come to this," Escandoza said, "but someone has to always pay a price. You two now, and your friend Gates when he realizes you are no more." He motioned to the guard to secure their ankles with the leg irons.

That was when the jungle started shaking. A rapid, thunderous drumming grew into a roar.

"Earthquake?" Candice asked Skyler.

"No," he said. "The cavalry."

Candice screamed as Castillo reached out and pushed her into the cenote. A second later, she pushed Skyler.

STOP AND BOARD

General Cho awoke with a start from a deep sleep. He sat up and swung his legs over the side of the bunk in the cramped cabin below decks. Something was wrong. The *Sunan* had stopped. No engine vibration, no rolling on the ocean swells, no motion at all— just silence. He stood, slipped his feet into his shoes and grabbed a shirt. He had slept in his pants. Pushing open the cabin door, he looked in both directions along the narrow passage before moving to the stairs leading topside.

He emerged into a blazing morning sun over a calm sea. Shielding his eyes from the glare, he looked toward the stern. Where were his men? Why wasn't the ship underway? With no one in sight, he moved toward the bow. Rounding the wheelhouse superstructure, he froze at the sight of his soldiers gathered on the forward deck in a tight grouping with their hands behind their heads. Then he saw the imposing form of a warship a hundred or so meters off the port bow.

"Good morning, General."

Cho turned to see a man in uniform step forward. Behind the officer, a group of armed U.S. Marines kept watch over the Korean soldiers.

"I'm Commander Thomas Marshall of the United States Navy and that is the guided missile destroyer USS *Lassen*. You have been stopped and boarded under the direct orders of the President. You and your men are to surrender immediately. You will be taken on board the *Lassen* and transported to the holding facility at Guantanamo Bay, Cuba. There you will be held until formal charges are made. Your ship will be handed over to the United States Coast Guard as evidence. Any questions?"

"I'm in the service of the Democratic People's Republic of Korea. I have diplomatic immunity. You have no right to detain me."

"You should have thought of that before you threatened the safety and security of the United States." The commander motioned and two Marines took Cho into custody.

The sun heated Cho's face as he felt a Marine secure his hands behind him with flexicuffs. He was assisted down a set of stairs on the side of the freighter to a motor launch. From his seat Cho watched the *Lassen* grow larger until it dominated his view. It was then that he realized other warships were nearby. He sucked in his breath knowing he would be a failure in the eyes of the General Secretary. His family dishonored. Even if he somehow gained his freedom from the Americans, there would be no going back to his home, his country. He felt suddenly alone surrounded by an unfriendly sea. He knew there was only one honorable thing left to do. He shot from his seat and dove over the gunwale into the dark Caribbean. Kicking with all his strength, he aimed his body straight down into the depths.

After ten meters, he blew out his breath, sucked seawater into his lungs and sank into oblivion.

HEAT SIGNATURE

"Try to turn around." Skyler treaded water beside Candice. When she did, he maneuvered so he could untie the rope binding her wrists, thankful there was not enough time for the guard to apply the leg irons. Once free, she did the same for him. They swam to the wall of the cenote and grabbed onto the ledge where he had slept the night before. "Are you okay?"

"I will be when I get my hands on that bitch that pushed me in."

"Maybe you'll get your chance. First, we've got to get out of here."

Skyler started searching for the strongest vines. As he did, the well echoed with the sound of a loud whoosh. A rocket shot across the sky above the canopy followed immediately by a Cobra gunship. "The attack on the island has started."

"What about Escandoza's threat?" Candice asked.

"He's just crazy enough." Skyler found and tested a thick vine. "This one should do."

The thumping of another helicopter filled the well—it sounded close by and didn't seem to be moving. In less than a minute, a rope appeared and dangled down the wall followed by the familiar, booming voice. "You gonna stay down there all morning?"

"Is that Mickey?" Candice asked.

"The one and only." He took the end of the rope and looped it under Candice's arms. "Hold on tight," he said and gave her a kiss. "I'll be right behind you." Then he swam to the middle of the cenote and signaled Gates to pull her up.

Soon the rope was thrown back down. This time, Skyler didn't wait to be pulled up, but instead used it to climb out. At the top, he took Candice into his arms and held her tight. Then he turned to his brother from a different mother. "How did you find us?"

"We knew where you were since last night from your heat signature." Gates pointed skyward. "Drone." They had to shout over the sound of the Seahawk hovering nearby. "Figured you were the only one that could wind up getting himself trapped in a sacrificial well."

"Thank you, my friend. Now let's get this party started." Skyler led Candice to where the cables from the Seahawk hung down in the clearing. Soon, the three, along with two Army Rangers, were skimming across the top of the jungle canopy toward columns of black smoke rising from the direction of the korium lab compound. The battle had been quick and destructive. Numerous bodies lay scattered about.

As the helicopter maneuvered in for a landing on the beach, Skyler saw a line of men being marched to waiting motor launches—Escandoza's men along with sailors from the *Tiger Shark* guarded by Rangers.

"Where are they taking them?" Skyler asked.

245

"Out to the *Iwo Jima* about eight kilometers to the east," Gates replied.

As they stepped out onto the sand, Candice started running toward the line of prisoners. "There she is!"

"Oh shit." Skyler took off after her with Gates right behind.

Teresa Castillo walked near the end of the line, her hands secured behind her. When she saw Candice charging toward her she froze with a shocked expression.

"You tried to kill us!" Candice screamed and came to a halt a few inches from her face.

The guards and prisoners stopped and turned to watch.

"How did you—"

"Escape?" Before Castillo could brace herself, Candice slapped her so hard that the woman lost her balance and dropped to the ground. A couple of Escandoza's men reacted with whoops and whistles as if they wanted to see more. Apparently, Castillo was not so popular with everyone in Escandoza's organization.

Skyler grabbed Candice and pulled her away, but not before she yelled, "That's just the beginning of what's in store for you in prison."

"Calm down, Candy." He held her so she couldn't go at Castillo again. "She'll get what's coming to her."

The guards helped Castillo to her feet, and the line began moving again.

"Damn, Candy," Gates said. "I always took you for being mild mannered and easy going. You slapped the crap out of her."

"Give me five more minutes with her and she'll need a plastic surgeon."

Gates turned to Skyler. "Remind me to never piss off your lady."

246

"Candy," Skyler said, "I'm going to arrange for you to be choppered out to the *Iwo Jima* where you'll be safe."

"I can take care of myself."

"You've established that. But this is still a hot zone. I'll feel better when you're safely on board the amphibious assault ship."

"But—"

"No buts." He took her by the arm and led her back to the Seahawk. "This will all be over soon and then we'll take a long vacation."

"As long as you promise that if you spot a Russian sub, you ignore it and come back to bed."

"Deal."

SWIM WITH THE TIDE

arine Super Cobra gunships whipped the air as Skyler and Gates walked across the sandy compound to the entrance gate of the korium lab, now a mass of twisted metal and tangled chain link fencing. The trade winds caught the smoke from the partially burned-out structure and swept it out to sea. The acidic smell of charred wood and cordite lingered. Among the Rangers guarding a rescue chopper was Captain Rees.

"I need to say goodbye to someone," Gates said, and trotted off in the direction of the aircraft. "I'll catch up with you."

Skyler watched him go. Then he turned and noticed a man a short distance away leaning against the thick trunk of a coconut palm. It was William Thorpe. His body sagged— his empty eyes stared into the distance.

"Glad to see you made it out in one piece, Dr. Thorpe." Skyler approached the scientist. "I'm Matt Skyler with OceanQuest."

Thorpe turned in Skyler's direction and sighed. "I know who you are, and that's one way of looking at it."

"Any way you look at it you still created a revolutionary new energy source."

"I created a monster, fed it, nurtured it, let it grow. I wound up building something evil. I can't believe I let it get this far."

"You didn't, Dr. Thorpe," Skyler said. "You just got caught up in the riptide. The secret to survival is knowing when to fight the current and when to swim with it until you're safely back on shore. You can be proud of what you did."

"So many could have died." Thorpe turned his eyes toward the horizon.

"Look at it this way. What does a Candle do? It gives off light, right?" Skyler placed a reassuring hand on the scientist's shoulder. "Remember your original goal with Project Candle Power—an alternative energy source? What's to stop you from completing it now? I'm told there's a great deal of korium still crated in the sub. Use it for the good of mankind."

Thorpe's eyes brightened as he looked at Skyler. "Maybe I still have time to make up for my foolishness. Do you think they will put me in prison?"

"I can't speak for the authorities, but I believe they'll realize that you're more valuable to the country and the world out of prison than in. And I happen to know some guys with an outfit called Deep Scan who would love to have you working for them. Just swim with the tide until you're safe on shore."

Thorpe stood a little taller. "I will." He extended his hand. "Thank you."

"If for no other reason," Skyler said as they shook, "I'm getting tired of paying the high prices at the gas pump."

Thorpe gave a timid smile and walked back in the direction of the temporary military command post.

That's when Skyler spotted Gates running toward him with a sat phone in his hand.

"What's up, Mick?

"This shit ain't over, Sky."

He saw the grave look on his best friend's face. "Explain."

"Escandoza's second sub—the *Mako Shark*—Blackstone is in command and threatening to launch a Candle at Los Angeles unless we release the drug lord."

"Where is Escandoza?"

"He was choppered out to the *Iwo Jima* about ten minutes ago. He's being held under guard until the military arranges for transport to Gitmo."

Skyler thought for a moment, then turned toward the command post. "Dr. Thorpe, wait up!"

The scientist paused.

Skyler raced to his side with Gates a few steps behind. "Doctor, I know you developed the process for turning korium into a major energy source. But did you have anything to do with the design of its implementation into the warhead?"

"Of course. Without my input, they would never have been able to make the adaption work."

"I see where you're going, Sky." Gates turned to Thorpe. "Is there a way to disarm the warhead?"

"I'm afraid not. Escandoza was specific in the design. Once it's armed and the launch code is activated, there's no turning back."

Skyler rubbed the stubble on his chin as he noticed an increase in activity around him. "Colonel," he called to the commander of the Marine assault team a few meters away.

The officer appeared to be in an intense sat phone conversation. He signed off and gave Skyler is attention.

"Mr. Skyler," he said walking toward the three men. "I only have a moment."

"What's going on?" Skyler asked.

"Washington has refused Blackstone's demands to release Escandoza. The launch of the Candle on Los Angeles is imminent."

"We may have a method to keep that missile from reaching LA. Have you transported Captain Schafer to the *Iwo Jima* yet?"

"About to. He's in the next group of prisoners."

"I need you to bring him down to the *Tiger Shark*. He's going to have to synchronize the missile control system with the one on Blackstone's sub."

"You mean you intend to blow up his Candle?"

"Exactly."

The Colonel narrowed his eyes at Skyler. "I'll have him there in five minutes." Then he started calling out a series of commands into his sat phone.

Skyler took Thorpe by the arm and led him in the direction of the wharf and the submarine. "Let's go swim with the tide, doctor."

FIRE CONTROL

Skyler, Gates and Dr. Thorpe squeezed in the missile guidance control room of the *Tiger Shark* as the Marine colonel brought in Captain Schafer.

"Good to see you again, Schafer," Skyler said.

"I wish I could say the same." Schafer was shoved into the tight compartment. "I can't imagine what you would want with me. I'm already your prisoner and you control my submarine."

"What we want should be easy for you," Skyler said. "Sit here." He patted the back of the fire control operator's chair. "I need you to synchronize this guidance system with the one on the *Mako Shark*."

Schafer's expression gave away that he realized what Skyler was going to attempt. "That's impossible. They're two separate systems, independent of each other."

"Not true," Skyler said. "Dr. Thorpe has assured me your boss requested redundant systems."

Schafer shot Thorpe a hard stare. "So much for loyalty among thieves."

"I owe my loyalty to no one," Thorpe said. "At least not anymore."

"Enough chitchat," Skyler said. "Captain, sit!"

Schafer took the fire-officer's chair, but remained stoic. "And if I refuse?"

Skyler motioned to the Marine's sidearm. The colonel slid the Beretta M9 from his holster and handed it over. Skyler pulled the slide back then placed the barrel's tip at the base of Schafer's' skull. "Then we'll have to wash your brains off the console before we find someone else to do the job." He hoped Schafer fell for his bluff—the sub's fire control office was already transported to the deck of the *Iwo Jima*.

Schafer glared at Skyler. "I should have had you shot when you dove off my deck." Then he slowly extended his hands over the keyboard. "I expect to be treated fairly for assisting you."

"Not my call," Skyler said. "But I hear Guantanamo Bay is lovely this time of year."

Schafer grunted, then began typing, causing the console to light up.

Skyler turned to Thorpe and motioned for the scientist to keep watch over the captain's shoulder. A monochrome CRT monitor displayed scrolling text that reminded Skyler of the old DOS commands from back in the day.

After what seemed like enough time for the captain to write a novel, he paused and leaned back in the chair. "The guidance control systems are in sync." He turned to face the small group. "But it appears you are too late."

Skyler yanked Schafer to his feet and shoved him toward the Marine. Then he turned to Thorpe. "You're up."

CRISIS CENTER

The President along with his national security team watched the large, high resolution monitor in the basement of the West Wing of the White House. Dr. Dolen, Professor Reynolds and Colonel Argentine were there as well. Everyone was focused on the monitor. It displayed the confirmation of an SLBM launch from approximately 1600 kilometers off the California coast. The projected course and target indicated Los Angeles.

"This is beyond belief," the President said. "General Greer, are we still at DEFCOM 3 from the first Candle launch?"

"Yes, sir," said the chairman of the Joint Chiefs of Staff.

"Take us to DEFCOM 2 and be ready to go to one in the event this attack opens a window of opportunity to others to strike at us."

Greer motioned to one of his aides who began nodding as he listened to the general's orders and inputted the info into a tablet.

The President turned to the three members of the Deep Scan team. "I thought you guys assured me that they had used up all their korium. That there couldn't be another Candle beyond the one they detonated over Hawaii."

"I'm afraid we got our estimates wrong," Dolen said.

"Not in how much korium was left, Mr. President," Reynolds said, "but in how little it takes to produce a fusion device."

"Its capacity to create energy is still being evaluated," Argentine added.

"Can't we shoot it down?" the President asked no one in particular.

"The interceptor missiles at Vandenberg are being readied, sir," Greer said. "But they can't be launched until the incoming warhead is in sight of the interceptor's associated radar."

"They better get ready fast." the President said. "That thing is already halfway to—"

"What the hell?" Alan Grant said as he got to his feet.

"What just happened?" The President's eyes stayed glued to the launch telemetry and projected path of the missile which seem to come to a grinding halt.

"It just . . . disappeared." Reynolds said.

"Maybe it exploded," Grant added.

"Is that possible?" the President asked.

No one answered for a moment.

Dean Clancy ended a call. "I have confirmation, Mr. President. The Candle blew up approximately three hundred miles off the California coast. Something caused the warhead to detonate during reentry into the lower atmosphere. The explosion was bright enough to be seen from as far away as our stations in Alaska."

The President stood. "General, launch your counter measures."

COUNTER MEASURES

Blackstone stood on the bridge of the *Mako Shark* and screamed, "What the fuck just happened?"

"We've lost contact, sir," the first officer said in a less than enthusiastic tone.

"You mean *lost contact* as in it's still on target but you aren't receiving telemetry, or you've lost control the missile?"

Before the first officer could answer, the fire control officer's voice came through the intercom speaker. "Guidance, Conn."

Blackstone pressed a button on the speaker housing. "Conn here. What the hell's going on?"

"Captain, the missile exploded as it came out of sub-orbit. The warhead detonated a few milliseconds later."

Blackstone rubbed his face. "How could that happen?"

There was a long pause. "Sir, someone synchronized our guidance control system with the one on the *Tiger Shark*."

"And?"

"They inputted the missile destruct code. Before we realized what happened and tried to override, it was too late."

"Then get us out of here fast before they find us."

The speaker box buzzed. "Conn, Sonar. High-speed screws, sir! Torpedoes in the water!"

"How many?"

"Two, sir. No wait. Three—now I count four."

"Crash dive!" Blackstone ordered. "Put us on the bottom. And start counter measures."

"More high-speed screws, sir!" The operator's voice cracked and wavered. "Two more torpedoes. They're from a second submarine."

Ping . . . ping . . . ping . . .

"Son of a bitch!" Blackstone grabbed a railing as the deck pitched forward.

"They've acquired us, captain!"

"Tell me something I don't know," Blackstone yelled back.

"One thousand yards and closing fast, sir."

"Brace for impact!" Blackstone announced through the PA system.

The *Mako Shark* shuddered as it raced downward.

"Can we outrun the torpedoes?" the first officer asked.

Blackstone smiled. "Not a chance."

U-396

S kyler looked up through his face mask at Candice waving at him from the rear deck of the *Pegasus*. In the blinding glare of the Caribbean noonday sun, he squinted as he waved back. Then he adjusted his mouthpiece and swam over to a bright orange buoy a few meters away. Gates treaded water nearby, his eyes wide with the same excitement from the thrill of the hunt, the quest for treasure. Every cell in his body was in overdrive as Skyler gave Gates a thumbs-up and grabbed the descent line connected to the buoy. In the next instance, Skyler was engulfed in an emerald world of shimmering sunbeams. The white nylon line faded into an endless expanse as he followed it down 47 meters to the ocean floor.

Skyler took his time pausing twice to clear his ears. When the bottom finally rose up and surrounded him, he adjusted his buoyancy compensator vest and checked his air pressure gauge. Gates arrived beside him and gave a thumbs up. Skyler noted the time on his watch and took a bearing from his wrist compass. He pointed to his right and started swimming across the flat sandy bottom. A few moments later, a V-shaped trench appeared in the dim light filtering through the clear water. Both men glided over the edge and dropped down along its side—a layered wall of limestone and coral—until they reached the bottom 10 meters below. Changing direction, they followed the trench for another minute or two.

Skyler had spent the morning studying records, photos, and blueprints from the Howarldtswerke AG shipyards in Kiel. Howarldtswerke built 31 U-boats between 1939 and 1944—U-396 was commissioned October 16, 1943. Originally it was reported sunk in April of 1945 in the North Atlantic southwest off the Shetlands by depth charges from a British Liberator. It was not until the post-Cold War archives suggested the Martin Bormann connection that Germany contracted OceanQuest to conduct a search.

U-396 was a 67-meter-long, VIIC-type diesel with five torpedo tubes—four in the bow and one at the stern. Like many VIIC's, 396 was fitted with a snorkel—a device allowing the boat to run its diesels submerged, giving it a significant boost in underwater speed over its electric motors. U-396 was also equipped with a powerful 3.5-inch deck cannon.

Running these details over in his mind, Skyler smiled as he saw the dark form of the U-boat materialize out of the shadows. It listed slightly, its keel fitting snugly in the bottom of the trench. As he swam up over the bow, he recognized the type VIIC features—it was one of the most common submarines in the German Kriegsmarine. The deck cannon, now swollen twice its original size with a heavy layer of coral and sponge, passed under him. He saw the conning tower looming ahead. Despite patches of marine growth encrusting it, he could make out parts of a number on its side—396. The control room and attack periscopes along with the snorkel still stood at attention atop the tower. The once-feared pride of the Third Reich had been converted into a home to parrot fish, spotted grouper, and yellow-tailed snapper along with thousands of other species of tropical marine life.

Skyler and Gates circled around the conning tower then swam along the port side. Halfway between the tower and the stern the trench opened slightly revealing a gaping cut about five meters long and a meter wide just below the boat's water line. Skyler knew it was the result of a collision with a large object, one of the many reefs dotting the area, no doubt. U-396 was probably running on the surface and could easily have been blown off course in a storm, struck the jagged teeth of a coral reef, and sunk fast—a terrible death for all on board.

He swung the lantern beam inside the opening and saw a huge metallic flash as the light reflected off a tightly packed school of tiny silverfish. With a nod toward Gates, he slipped through the opening into the galley. Moving past the oddly deformed shapes of the stove and pantry, he edged his way down a narrow passage. Within a few meters, a watertight door blocked his progress—closed and sealed—standard procedure in a time of crisis. Skyler tested the heavily encrusted unlocking wheel but it was hopelessly frozen.

He saw a partially opened door to his left leading to what he knew was the small captain's cabin. If Bormann had been on board, such a VIP would undoubtedly have been given use of this accommodation. He pushed hard, managing to open the space just enough to squeeze through. Shining his lantern beam around the compact quarters, he recognized a writing desk, some pigeonhole storage slots above it, and to the side what was once a bunk. A dark space attracted his attention beneath the bed.

He moved closer, brought the beam down, and shined it toward the space. There was a mass of sponges, and a grandfather-size lobster stood his ground for a moment before scurrying across the floor, leaving Skyler alone.

He swung the beam closer. Suddenly, in a streak of shimmering, undulating silver ribbon, prehistoric-like teeth, and empty black eyes, a moray shot out, striking the lantern with such a force it knocked the lamp from Skyler's hand. Stopping only to reclaim its ground, the moray struck the light again.

As Skyler recoiled, a shaft shot across the light beam and impaled the eel. The deadly barbs of the spear stuck out of the side of the monster as Gates moved into the cramped cabin, pushing the body of the dead creature out of the way with the end of the spear gun.

Skyler gestured a grateful OK, and turned back to retrieve his lantern. It was then that he saw a handle attached to what appeared to be a small suitcase or attaché case. With a bit of hesitation, not knowing if the eel had a roommate, he reached to grab the handle. A chill ran through him as he pulled the heavily encrusted metal case from underneath the bunk. Bones, perhaps human, drifted out in the smoky swirls of its wake. First, a femur, then a few vertebrae, and finally a skull rolled in slow motion out of the sediment. Skyler took the skull, examined it, and handed it to Gates. With a firm grip on the case, he looked at his watch then motioned upwards. Gates nodded and they started back through the cabin door.

Out of the jagged wound in the side of U-396, the two men emerged and glided across the crusty deck of the boat and up the wall of the trench. They paused for a moment at the base of the buoy line before beginning the recommended one-foot-per-second ascent.

Skyler felt the heavy case pull against him almost as if it were reluctant to reenter the world of the living. Finally breaking the surface, he waved to the group gathered on the stern of the *Pegasus* a dozen meters away. He pulled the mouthpiece from his teeth and shouted, "Toss down a basket." Seconds later, they dropped a metal frame basket over the side. With Gates' help, Skyler hoisted the case in and carefully placed the skull beside it. Then Skyler motioned to the crew to pull it up. Soon, the two men sat on the dive platform slipping off their tanks and belts.

"Thanks, Mick." Skyler patted his friend on the back. "That moray caught me totally by surprise. I was distracted with the idea of feasting on that lobster."

"Good thing it went for the lantern and not your arm." Gates ran his fingers through his thick hair. "So who do you think that skull belonged to?"

"Good question. That's why I love this job. There's always another mystery to solve." Skyler beamed with a smile as broad as a young boy's on Christmas morning.

The two stood and headed up the ladder to the deck of the converted Coast Guard Cutter. A group had already gathered around the two prizes, inspecting and probing. Candice greeted Skyler with a kiss and slipped her arm around his waist as they strolled across the deck.

"This just keeps getting better and better, Sky," called the heavily accented voice of Chief Inspector Walter Smyth. The pudgy little Englishman stood in sandals, a bright Hawaiian shirt and shorts, dark sunglasses and a straw hat. He offered Skyler, Candy and Gates each a cold beer.

"You're right, Inspector. Let's hope we're not disappointed." Skyler downed half his beer in one gulp.

"I'm so glad you insisted I come on vacation to the Caribbean." Smyth beamed. "Sure beats Greenland."

"No chance of freezing to death here." Gates wiped the cold beer can across his brow.

Skyler moved over to the table where the skull and case lay. The case was encrusted with marine life and mud but seemed intact. After an initial inspection, he had a crewman retrieve a wire brush. Using it, he removed the layers of sediment.

"Aluminum," Gates said as the brush quickly exposed the metal surface.

"And look what we have here." Skyler's brush strokes revealed markings in the upper right corner—the faint image of an Eagle with its wings spread. Below it was the unmistakable symbol of the Nazi swastika. Finally, engraved below the emblem of the Third Reich, were the initials: A.H.

A hush fell over the group as Skyler tried the two clamps holding the lid shut. They resisted. A crewman handed the marine explorer a screwdriver, and with a bit of force, the first clamp snapped open. Then the other. Slowly, he raised the lid.

The ocean seemed to calm, the breeze stilled, the clouds faded into the deep blue of the sky, and the bright Caribbean sun blazed down, reflecting off the brilliant surface of twelve gold bars.

~~~

Two days later, having conducted a thorough search of U-396, the OceanQuest crew spent the last evening celebrating and enjoying the warm Caribbean night. Tomorrow, the *Pegasus* would sail for Key West and their next assignment.

Skyler stood at the stern railing of the ship, his arm around Candice Stevens. She looked up at his rough and weathered face. He smiled down at her and held her tight.

"The German authorities must have been ecstatic when you told them about the gold," she said.

"By today's prices, it's only worth a couple million dollars. However, its real value to collectors is tenfold, maybe a hundred-fold. If the Germans sell it, the proceeds will go a long way in the efforts to repay the Holocaust survivors."

"And the skull? Who do you really think it is?"

"I have no idea. Could be the captain, a crewman . . . "

"Or Martin Bormann?"

Skyler shrugged. "We may never know, Candy."

The stars glistened off the dark water as the research ship rolled on the gentle swells.

"Sky?"

He turned to see Gates coming across the deck toward them. "What's up, Mick?"

"A fax from the Frankfurt justice officials. The courier delivered the skull yesterday afternoon. A forensic science professor from Munich University conducted preliminary tests. He had Bormann's dental and medical records on file."

"And?" Skyler asked.

"It's not Bormann."

"So who then?" Candice said.

"Well, the commander of U-396 was Hilmar Siemon, so he's out. I checked the crew roster, there were 44 souls, none with the initials A.H."

Then Candice said, "Do you suppose A.H. could stand for . . .?"

There was a long silence as Skyler and Gates stared at each other.

"Nah," they finally said in unison with a chuckle.

Skyler glanced one last time over the rail at the buoy that marked the final resting-place of U-396. Then he turned around, "Sounds like we're missing a good party."

Arm-in-arm, the three headed across the deck in the direction of Calypso music and laughter.

To learn more about Joe Moore, visit
http:www.sholesmoore.com

www.ingramcontent.com/pod-product-compliance
Lightning Source LLC
Chambersburg PA
CBHW072211170626
46813CB00003B/892